MANDY

Fishboy

A magical underwater adventure

Mandy Collins worked as an advertising executive in London in the 80's and more recently trained as a Yacht Surveyor. She lives by the creek in Conyer, North Kent with her husband and two Tibetan Terriers writing in her spare time. This is her second book.

Magellan House Publishing
ISBN: 978-0-9935706-0-5

Chapters

Simon,

What would your dream of a
childhood adventure be?

This would be mine.

And I hope it will
be yours!

Mandy Collins.

CHAPTER 1 – Another Beautiful Day

It was another beautiful day at Lazy Haze beach and Bruno was standing as still as he could on the rocks in his swimming trunks, casually holding onto his new birthday fishing rod. He'd already been fishing loads of times this holiday and so far hadn't had a bite, but he was still hopeful, and felt quite grown up with the rod in his hand.

Suddenly, a head popped up next to his line. Bruno was so surprised; he lost his balance and fell sideways into the sea.

'Where did you come from?' he cried out between breaths. The boy was looking at him. 'Oh, I've been here for ages, diving for shells.' Bruno frowned. He'd been fishing from these rocks now for more ages than his new friend, he thought, and hadn't seen anyone swimming out from the beach.

'Oh, did you find any good ones?' he asked whilst treading water.

The boy nodded and shyly lifted out of the water a green net, the size of a football, which was full of beautiful shells in all shapes and sizes. Bruno opened his mouth in amazement at the haul, and forgot that he was treading water. Immediately, his whole body started sinking downwards, his mouth filled with seawater, and his ears started to hum. He kicked his legs to power him to the surface, and as he moved upwards he saw a dark shape moving quickly away and down into the depths.

When he had finished coughing and spluttering, the boy had gone.

Bruno's auntie lived in Cornwall, married to the managing director of the local airport. They lived in a beautiful, large pink house overlooking the beach. One of those magical houses where as a 10 year old, you would be allowed to disappear for a couple of hours whereas at home, you would always be asked, 'Where are you going?' or 'What are you doing?' Every year, Bruno, with his younger sister, Paisley, and both parents would spend a week here, and then his parents would go back home to Surrey, and the children would stay for another blissful 5 weeks. Auntie Moo, as she was called, was odd and eccentric. She had never had any children and filled this place in her life with a horrible big black cat called Bosun, or better known as Horror Pet.

It was the second week of the holiday, and Bruno was just beginning to relax. His Mum was pretty strict with him and when she was around, he had to watch himself. Strangely, his

Aunt didn't seem to mind much about his manners and behaviour and provided he told her when he would be back, there were no questions asked. She had taken Paisley into Oldquay for the morning to do some shopping and Bruno had agreed that he would meet them on the beach for lunch.

His cousin, who was 2 years older than Bruno, was staying with them this year and they had gone down to the beach early. They both attended the same school and whilst there was an age difference, they got on well and enjoyed the same things. Both were blond with blue eyes and could have been taken for brothers

'Hamish, guess what just happened to me?' Bruno shouted as he splashed through the surf and up the beach. 'I saw this strange boy who had all these fantastic shells and then… well… I nearly drowned, and he seemed to disappear.' Bruno was panting, through excitement and lack of breath. Hamish looked at Bruno and smiled. He knew his cousin wouldn't have made this up. Bruno was too serious for that. Hamish had noticed that at school and at his own home Bruno behaved in a very grown up way - looking after Paisley, mixing well with all their parent's friends, and being anxious to please.

Hamish teased him that sometimes he behaved like his own father. So it was great to see him laughing and relaxing here.

'He couldn't have disappeared,' said Hamish still with a smile on his face. 'He's probably just hiding. Come on, let's have a look.'

They ran back into the surf and clambered up onto the outcrop of rocks, which protruded out into the bay. The rocks were easy to climb and it didn't take the boys long to reach the water's edge where Bruno had seen the boy.

They hadn't passed anybody and couldn't see anything in the water. Suddenly, a dark shape swam towards them and the boy appeared as if he had come from the depths below. Bruno waved. 'Hello again.' The boy waved and swam in closer. He looked older than they were and had very dark hair and dark eyes to match. He was quite thin and wore some strange swimming trunks. Bruno thought they looked as if they had been made out of seaweed.

Bruno helped him out onto the rocks. The net with the shells was nowhere to be seen.

'I was just telling my friend about your shells. Have you lost them?'

The other boy looked embarrassed. 'Oh, no, I took them home.' He smiled. His straight white teeth breaking through his suntanned face. 'But I can bring them to show you another time, if you like.'

'OK, cool, where do you live then?' asked Bruno, relieved that he hadn't dreamt the boy and the shells.

'A couple of miles from here. It's called Marino, but I doubt whether you'll have heard of it. I'm afraid I'm not allowed to invite friends over, but we could arrange to meet tomorrow.' He paused. 'Do you have a boat?'

'Well, I could borrow my aunt's sailing dinghy.' Bruno replied. 'Where shall we meet?'

The boy lifted his right arm and drew a small arc towards the side of the bay. 'There is a cave around the corner from where we are. It's not that far but very difficult to find, unless you know it. But you can sail right into it, and we could meet there. Just look out for the butterflies. They'll show you the way. I've got to go. See you then at high tide tomorrow.' The boy dived into the water almost without a splash, and Bruno and Hamish cast their eyes around to wait for him to surface. After a while, Hamish looked at Bruno frowning. 'Who was that?'

'I don't know,' said Bruno excitedly, 'but we must be there at high tide. I think it's about 11.00.'

CHAPTER 2 – A Strange Meeting

Bruno knew all about tides. His Aunt had taught him to sail a couple of years earlier, and explained all about them. How they are controlled by the pull between the earth, the moon and the sun and how the time of the high tide changes every day. It moves forward approximately by one hour. There are also very high tides when there is a new moon and when there is a full moon. These are called 'Spring Tides.' There are also other times when the high tide level is very low and these are called 'Neap Tides.'

The next day, there was a spring tide which would mean they would have lots of time either side of high water in which to launch the boat and return before the tide disappeared out for miles making it difficult to drag the boat up the beach.

The boys were lent the boat on the usual conditions:

- Wear a lifejacket at all times.
- Wear at least a shorty wet suit to keep the wind off whilst sailing.
- Never leave the boat
- Return by 4.00

Their excitement was obvious, but Auntie

Moo assumed this to be because of their love of sailing. She was pleased that the boys enjoyed the sport. Bruno had really taken to it and become an excellent helmsman, whilst Hamish was happy to be his crew. Sailing had been an obsession of Auntie Moo's since she was a young child, and she couldn't understand how some people hated it.

It was a warm sunny day, with a calm sea and a gentle breeze. Bruno and Hamish had breakfast and hurried into the boat shed next door to the house, to collect the rigging and sails for the dinghy. Everything was bundled into an old wheelbarrow and Hamish took charge. The path down to the beach was steep but sandy, so it was easy to control the wheelbarrow, even though Bruno didn't help by getting into it at intervals giving his friend a heavier load.

The boat was an 11ft clinker built sailing dinghy called Wishful. It was very stable and ideal for children on their own. The boys rigged the dinghy carefully, and then pushed the trailer into the water until it was deep enough for the dinghy to be floated off. Bruno was so excited; he forgot to put on his lifejacket and had to do this with one hand, once in the boat, as the wind had already caught the sails. His other hand was on the tiller, steering the boat seawards.

They left the outcrop of rocks on their right, and soon passed the headland point where they turned right to follow the cliffs.

'I can't see a cave along here,' said Hamish squinting through the sun. 'I suppose this could be a joke, you know.'

Bruno shrugged. 'It doesn't matter, this is fun anyway.' Hamish could tell that it did matter and that Bruno was already a bit embarrassed at believing the boy's tale about the cave.

The cliffs were so high that you had to put your head right back to see the top. There was no break in them, and certainly no cave. Bruno decided to sail in very close to see if they were missing anything.

'Look over there - butterflies,' cried Hamish. A long train of small blue and yellow butterflies were flapping silently towards them. The train turned just ahead of the dinghy and flew off to the right as if they were going straight for the rocks. 'Quick, follow them,' shouted Hamish. Bruno frowned. They were already too close in for his liking. 'OK, but we need to be ready to take the sails down.'

Bruno turned the boat and followed the butterflies that had by now reached the cliff face. The train had turned left and as the boys watched, the beginning of the line started to disappear as if they had flown behind a wall. 'There it is. That must be the entrance to the cave. Let's go,' shouted Hamish.

Bruno swung the tiller over, and the little dinghy slowly headed towards the place where the butterflies had disappeared, while Hamish took the jib down and prepared the oars. As they were about to touch the cliff face, they saw a crack opening up to their left. This would only ever be seen if you were right up against the cliff face, and would never be found without help. Bruno turned Wishful into the small opening; at the same time Hamish let the mainsail down and took one of the oars, which he would use as a paddle for the moment. Wishful carried on gliding forward through the opening.

Hamish had turned his head upwards, his mouth open in amazement. Whilst the opening to the cave was tiny, inside, the roof lifted right up and although the light was dim, you could see that the cave was very high and quite wide. There was enough room for three or four dinghies to moor up alongside a low ledge that ran from one side of the cave to the other. But the best part was the reflection from the sand underneath which gave the whole cave a turquoise blue glow that the boys had never seen before. Before they could say anything a voice addressed them.

'So you found it alright. Do you want to pass me a rope?' The boy was sitting on the ledge dangling his feet in the water. Bruno was the first one to reply, his voice shaking with excitement. 'Yes, the butterflies - Its amazing, how did you find it?'

'My family have lived around here for centuries. We know all the secret places. But it's a long story really, when do you need to be back?'

By 4 o clock, so need to leave here at 3.00 at the latest,' said Bruno responsibly.

The boy nodded. 'My name is Finlay, called Finn for short.' The boys introduced themselves and passed a rope over to Finn who tied it to one of a number of iron rungs set into the ledge. The boys clambered over the sails and ropes now lying in the bottom of the boat, and out onto the ledge.

'So, what's the story?' asked Hamish a little impatiently. He didn't know quite what to make of this new friend and was keen to find out more. Finn took a big sigh and flicked back his dark fringe. His big brown eyes shone out as he started to speak. His story was told in a matter of fact sort of way, which was a bit surprising seeing as what he was saying was almost unbelievable

'I come from an unusual race of people who have the ability to breath underwater. We are called Gillanders. I won't tell you the background now but obviously this means we are quite different to you. We have learnt to keep ourselves to ourselves although we mix with "Leylanders" which is our name for normal people. We are very independent. We have made ourselves a place to live, more an underwater village really, with all the usual things that you have but just different. The reason I wanted to talk to you is that our home could soon be ruined, and we don't feel we can do anything about it without Leylanders' help.'

'Phew,' said Hamish quickly. 'I'm not sure I believe all this. How long has this underwater village been built?'

'I don't know exactly but ever since my grandparents have been alive,' answered Finn with a serious expression on his face.

'And how many people live there?' asked Bruno. Finn shrugged his shoulder. 'It varies, but about 40 are there most of the time.'

'How do we know you're telling the truth?' Hamish exclaimed accusingly.

Finn stood up. He was as tall as Hamish, but much thinner. His body was tanned all over and there were no shoe sun tan marks on his feet, unlike both the boys who whilst spending all day in the sun, had marks from their beach shoes which they needed to climb over rocks. Finn lifted his left arm. Just above his waist there was a flap of skin in the shape of a 'U' approximately 1 inch across. There was another about 6 inches above that.

'These enable me to breathe underwater. I have one lung on the other side and on this side, I have fins like a fish.' He spoke quietly as if he knew that the sight of these fins might frighten the boys. Hamish took a step back and stood beside Bruno. He said nothing.

'Okay then,' exclaimed Bruno. 'Show us how you can swim without coming up for air. Give us the proof.'

'I'm glad you said that, young man,' said a voice from behind. Bruno jumped and turned to see an old man standing in front of them. He wore what Bruno thought was a 'shorty' wetsuit, but soon realised it was just a piece of strange material, cut like a wetsuit, that covered his body. He had a white beard but no hair on his head, and Bruno thought he looked the oldest man he'd ever seen.

'I don't want you to be startled,' said the old man raising his arm in a sort of welcome gesture. 'I can see that I have alarmed you.

Please sit down. We are friendly people and will not harm you.'

Bruno and Hamish sat down on the ledge and dangled their legs over the side into the bright blue water. They looked at each other but neither said anything. The old man continued. 'We have never told any Leylanders about ourselves before so we are as nervous of you as you will be of us. It is only our current situation that means we have to ask for help and that means being honest. Before I tell you the whole story, would you like to come and see our home? That might make you feel happier about listening to me.'

Both boys nodded at once although they didn't mean to. Bruno wanted to go home really, but had this funny feeling inside him, which was excitement and fear all in one. He knew that whilst his Aunt was easy going and never told him off, she would be furious if she had any idea where he was now.

The old man introduced himself. 'My name is Polperro and I have something for you.' He gave them each a pair of rubbery boots. 'These are called Aquadaptors and you will be able to breathe underwater whilst you are wearing them. When we get to the house, you will be able to take them off, as we will go into one of the 'breathable' rooms. Are you both all right?'

He knelt down and looked at their faces individually. His face was very lined, and suntanned, but it was a kind face and his voice was gentle. Hamish smiled and stood up slowly. 'Well, I'm up for it!' he said firmly.

Bruno looked uncertain. He was still worrying about his Aunt and whether Polperro was telling the truth. He realised he was being a bit pathetic as well, which irritated him as Hamish was being brave and adventurous, and he wanted to feel the same way. 'Okay, me too,' he said slowly.

They both sat down and pulled on their rubber boots. They looked like Wellington boots, but were soft like wet suit boots and as easy to pull on as a pair of socks. Bruno was waiting for something to happen, but he felt fine and stood up.

'Wait. What about Pluto?' Hamish pulled a large lizard out of his pocket. 'He can only stay underwater for an hour at a time.' Pluto was Hamish's pet Australian Water Dragon. He was a beautiful looking lizard with a red and green body and a large head. Hamish was obsessed with reptiles and had been given Pluto for his tenth birthday. The lizard went everywhere with him.

Finn took Pluto from Hamish and stroked him as if he was used to these sorts of reptiles.

'He'll be fine. The journey won't be as long as that and once you're at Marino, he'll be able to breathe again.'

He handed the lizard back to Hamish who beamed and pushed Pluto back into his pocket again.

Polperro explained, 'If you drop down into the water with Finn, he will show you out of the cave where you'll find we have laid on some personal water taxis for you.' He smiled. 'They are dolphins called Osquirt and Botolph. Both perfectly safe and used to having inexperienced riders on their backs.'

Hamish and Bruno didn't answer so he continued. 'The best way to ride a dolphin is to hold onto the top fin letting your legs lie out behind you towards their tail. This way you don't interfere with the way they move through the water, and they can still move quickly. Hold on tight. It may take you a little time to get used to it.'

Hamish and Bruno couldn't believe their ears. They looked at each other and raised their eyes in excitement, and then at Finn who was standing quietly behind Polperro. Bruno nodded at him.

Finn leapt into the water, followed by Hamish who held his breath as he disappeared under the surface, and then came back to the surface to wait for Bruno.

'Just put your head underwater slowly and start breathing normally. You shouldn't notice any difference,' explained Finn.

Hamish held onto the ledge with one hand and bobbed his head under. He was sure he would come up spluttering with a lungful of water, but was willing to try it. He opened his eyes and saw Finn in front of him smiling. His brown hair waving about in front of his eyes. Finn was gesticulating with his right hand towards his own mouth, opening it and obviously breathing in, raising his head slightly as he did so.

Hamish closed his eyes tightly, opened his mouth and breathed in. Nothing happened or rather something did happen. He was breathing normally. His 'Wow!' underwater came out differently but otherwise he could breathe. He bobbed his head back up out of the water where Bruno was treading water beside him.

'It works,' he shouted. 'It's like magic. Try it! 'Bruno couldn't not try it after that and ducked his head down. Both Hamish and Finn were by this time swimming around under him and he took a breath. His mind was full of questions and worries but right now he was in heaven. Bruno was the best swimmer in his class and competed in county competitions. Water was his home. To be able to explore beneath the surface was a dream come true. Hamish tapped him on the arm. Finn was pointing to the mouth of the cave and they all set off. Bruno very quickly catching up with Finn.

CHAPTER 3 – Marino

They swam through the gap and then Finn signalled to dive deeper. Bruno looked all around him. He could see a brightness above where the sun was shining on the water. Below was yellow sand, with rocks and pink coral covered in bright green seaweed. There were fish of all sizes swimming in and out of the coral and in the distance he could see the shape of a dolphin. He could feel his heart beating stronger, and worried that it might put the dolphin off. As he got closer, the dolphin turned towards him and came right up to Bruno so that he could stroke his nose. It felt hard and cold and a bit like a smooth piece of leather. The dolphin was moving his head around against Bruno's hand and looked like he was enjoying himself.

As instructed, Bruno got onto the dolphin's back and held tight onto his dorsal fin. Hamish copied him with the other dolphin and Finn swam between the two, with one hand on each dolphin so that he was carried along in the middle. The two dolphins swam as one, almost as if they were bolted together. They were careful to swim straight so as not to fling their passengers around, but they moved so easily through the water, neither boys had any problem hanging on. Both had large grins across their faces, although Bruno was wondering if this was all a dream and he would soon wake up. He noticed that Pluto had escaped from Hamish's pocket and was happily swimming alongside them looking very handsome.

The group moved swiftly across the sea bed, across the sand and into deeper water, they saw coral waving in the tide with millions of small fish feeding off the edge of the reef. A small octopus passed by and Hamish thought he felt a slap on his arm from one of its tentacles. They passed a mother and baby seal frolicking on the sea bed, and once or twice were surprised by puffins appearing from nowhere, diving down from above to pick up their lunch, snatching a small fish and then shooting back out of the water as quickly as they had arrived. The colours turned from being clear and bright to darker and dull. They were getting deeper and Bruno noticed the dolphins were slowing down. They were now close to the seabed, which was covered in rocks, and Bruno thought he could see where the seabed ended and then nothing – just a big hole. His experience so far had been wonderful and he had forgotten about his Aunt and the sailing dinghy now left miles behind, but suddenly he became anxious. He couldn't see where they were going to go anymore. His heart started racing. They were now very close to the ledge where there appeared to be nothing beyond. It was as if they were about to go over the edge of a cliff. The dolphins slowed right down and Bruno could see something far below them.

Marino had been built of grey slate without any cement. The Gillanders had built it using the dry wall method, piling slate pieces on top of each other to form a wall. Each slate piece had to be heavy enough to resist the tide and rough water. The house was enormous with turrets and windows, which reminded Bruno of a castle. There were many different parts to it that looked as if they had been added on at some stage. As they started to get nearer, he noticed a big balcony running down one side of the house.

The dolphins approached the balcony and as the group got closer a large glass door slid sideways opening into a plain, round, steel chamber. There was a rail around the chamber and nothing else. The dolphins swam into the chamber and stopped, where Finn, using sign language, showed that he wanted the boys to take hold of the rail. The boys obediently did as they were shown, and once free the dolphins turned and left the chamber. The door slid across, and a loud noise filled the chamber. At the same time Bruno noticed that the water was starting to drain out of the bottom and he could see air above. As the water was sucked out, the boys were pulled downwards and found a series of rails running down the wall. By standing on one they were able to stay in the same position until their heads surfaced. Hamish just managed to grab Pluto before he disappeared down the plughole.

'That was so cool,' said Hamish blinking and shaking his head. Bruno nodded and said, 'I still think I'm dreaming.'

'Well, just wait until you see our home, there are lots more surprises to come.' Said Finn proudly as he watched the last of the water disappear out of the bottom of the chamber.

They all climbed upwards using the rails around the chamber, and came out into a large room made of stone, but filled with brightly coloured wooden furniture that looked as if it had been made in one of Bruno's own carpentry lessons. He laughed to himself. They had a bit to learn here, he thought. There were two doors leading out of the room, both closed, and there were no windows, but the room felt homely. There were benches in a square, an enormous wooden dining table with chairs, a bookcase full of old books, and the most surprising thing of all, a large television.

One of the doors opened and Polperro walked in. Hamish noticed some movement behind him and looked down to see seven giant crabs, all racing along in a line behind him. 'Don't mind my friends, they like to spend a bit of their day out of the water, and down at this depth, they don't get the opportunity very much, so we let them wander around from time to time.'

Hamish and Bruno nodded, as if they were beginning to understand that life in Marino was quite different and full of surprises. Nothing seemed out of the ordinary down here, and they were beginning to relax. 'You could let Pluto have a run around with them if you like.' Polperro smiled at Hamish, who pulled the surprised looking lizard out of his pocket and placed him on the floor. Polperro continued.

'Are you cold? We can give you a towel whilst we dry off your wetsuits for you. We have turbo dryers that can dry those out in minutes.' Both boys nodded and started to peel off their wetsuits.' Bruno noticed that his waterproof watch was still working despite the depth and experience. It was midday. The whole journey had only taken 30 minutes.

Polperro continued, 'Would you like some lunch, we've got eel and snails today, either hot or cold with some seaweed and butter.'

Bruno only just managed to stop himself saying 'Yuck' out loud, and had to swallow deeply to stop himself from being sick at the thought of it.

Finn saw his discomfort. 'Polperro, could we have some hot, cooked prawns today as it is a special occasion. I hate eels and snails too.'

Polperro looked at the boys and grunted. 'You young boys are always so fussy. In my day, we ate what we were given and that was that. Ok, I'll ask the Fishers what they have got in today. You may have to make do with brown shrimps.' Polperro left the room, and the three boys looked at each other and burst into laughter. All anxiety had left Bruno and he felt as if he was at one of his friend's home for lunch.

'Come on, I'll introduce you to my father,' said Finn excitedly. 'Its not often that we have visitors down here, so he'll be very pleased to meet you.' The three boys filed out of the door after Finn into a narrow stainless steel corridor. There were no windows. Simply one door that was locked by a large wheel which Finn turned. This opened the door into another long corridor but the left wall was made of glass. Finn pointed to the room behind the glass. 'This is our aqasium.'

The room appeared to have walls made of brick, but was full of water. From the wall at the other end of the room, facing them, you could see a large hole, which seemed to be pumping water out and into the room. There was a young man trying to swim towards the hole but despite how hard he tried he couldn't beat the strong force of the water.

'That's our aquaspout. Only the fittest of the men here can swim against it. I can just about hold my position in the water now. But it's still very hard,' he explained.

'What's that in the corner?' Hamish was looking at a sort of bicycle. Another man was sitting on it; only his feet were strapped into large rubber plates instead of pedals. 'Weird,' added Hamish.

'That's the sea bike. Its used in the gym as a keep fit bicycle, but we also have some on the outside which we can use to pedal up to Oldquay if we want to exercise our legs.' He laughed. 'You see Gillanders don't use all their leg muscles whilst swimming so it's important to exercise them for when we need to walk on dry land.'

A third man was sitting inside a sort of tunnel on what looked like a dinghy complete with oars. He was rowing.

'And this is our rowing machine which keeps

our arm muscles fit. Its much harder to row underwater than it is on the surface.' Finn knocked on the glass and the man looked round and waved. He let his body float out of the rowing machine and swam over to the door. Bruno noticed a glass box, like a hallway between the room and the corridor. The man swam into it. Pressed a button and the water level started to fall. Once it had drained away, he opened the door to the corridor and stepped out.

His hair was long, down to his shoulders and it was jet black. His eyes were also very dark and Bruno noticed that his suntan through his seaweed suit was also darker than usual. He had a tattoo on his arm in the shape of a lobster.

'Welcome to Marino,' he said gently. 'Finn has told me all about you. I expect all this is a bit of a surprise, isn't it?'

'This is my father, Talon,' said Finn before the boys could answer. He is the main fisherman for the family.'

'How do you do,' said Bruno politely, nodding his head at Talon. 'What sort of fish do you catch?' he added, hoping he might get some help on why he had never managed to catch anything.

'We catch anything and everything that the Ocean offers. The fish and animals living in the sea are our friends though, and we both share this underwater world, so we try to catch only enough to feed us and make a living. We don't use large nets. Why don't you come out with me one day?'

'Oh yes,' answered Bruno. 'I'd love that.'

'We'll organise it next time you visit. Meanwhile I'd better be getting changed for lunch.' Talon turned and walked back towards the room that the boys had just left. Bruno noticed a large sign above the door "Breathable Room."

The boys made their way down the corridor away from the Breathable Room and Finn opened a door on the other side set into the steel wall. It opened up into another corridor where the wall on the right was replaced by a large glass panel. Inside was another room filled with water. It had a large wooden bed, which was tied with rope to 4 rings set in the stone floor. The bed was suspended in the middle of the room, and on the bed there lay a sea weed blanket that was obviously so heavy, it didn't move at all despite the slight swaying of the bed with the movement of the water. The room was teeming with small fish and just as Bruno had got close enough to press his nose to the glass, a large, dark shape came into view.

A shark was circling the room, its great jaw

passing in front of their eyes within inches as it continued its rounds. Bruno's hands went sticky with fear although he thought it was excitement.

'Bono is nothing to worry about.' Finn reassured them. 'He is one of our fast water taxis, and I left my door open, so he feels it's all right to come in. I normally close it when I'm sleeping, but look around the room further, there are many of my other friends in there.'

Up till now Bruno had just taken in the whole thing, which was really awesome. Now, he started to look in detail, he could see a mass of marine life all over the room. Starfish stuck to the walls, anemones covered all 4 corners. Beautiful sea urchins in all colours were scattered over the floor. There were crabs scuttling between them and 2 lobsters fighting under the bed. But the last thing that Bruno noticed was the turtle, as big as a dinner plate, sleeping on the seaweed at the foot of Finns bed.

'That's Consommé; she's been with me since she was tiny. She needs warmish water and we heat the water in our rooms a little as we've all become a bit soft over the years, so she's happy here. She's very loyal, and protects me from any crabs or lobsters that try to nibble my toes in the middle of the night. Hang on, I'll go and get her.'

Finn disappeared through one of the doors on the other side of the corridor, and after a few minutes Bruno and Hamish watched him swim into his bedroom. He was a good swimmer, but Bruno noticed his stroke was haphazard. At school Bruno had been taught crawl, breaststroke and butterfly, but Finn was using his legs in a sort of butterfly stroke and his arms in a breaststroke fashion. The combination resulted in a quick and sleek movement. Finn stopped swimming over the top of the turtle and gently picked her up. She poked her head out quickly and seemed happy to see Finn, who by this time was swimming back through the door.

He arrived in the corridor, soaking wet, a couple of minutes later with the turtle in his arms and handed him to Hamish. The turtle pulled her head back into its shell, and simultaneously a spurt of liquid shot out from her other end. Hamish laughed and quickly handed her back to Finn, wiping his hands on his towel.

'Sorry, she must be in bad mood.' Finn explained. 'She is sometimes when she has just woken up. Why don't you go back to the Breathable lounge? I expect everyone will be in there for lunch by now, and I'll put Consommé back.'

Everyone else, thought Bruno, how many others are there? The worrying feeling returned. He nodded and he and Hamish walked back down the corridor.

CHAPTER 4 – A moving feast

Bruno could hear a babble of voices coming from the Breathable Room as they approached the door. It was full of people of all ages. Men, women and children and all with dark brown hair. Most of the children wore swimming things, but the adults wore a similar outfit to that of Polperro. A sort of shorty wetsuit but in a seaweed material. Talon was there and joined them.

Polperro came forward. He raised his arms to quieten down the noise. 'People of Marino, please welcome Bruno and Hamish.' The crowd clapped and smiled, and then turned back to each other to continue chatting.

'They don't get the chance to talk to each other much. Only when we meet here for special occasions, so they have a lot to catch up on.' Polperro said smiling. 'Come along boys.' He waved his arms by his side. 'There are some free places next to me at the top of the table.'

They took their places either side of Polperro who was standing at the top of the long dining table. Finn stood beside Bruno, and Talon beside Finn. Everyone else took their places behind their chairs and looked towards Polperro, who closed his eyes.

'Thank you Godolphin, for watching over

our people and our seas, and for the food that we take from your kingdom.'

'Amarino,' was muttered quickly as chairs were pulled back.

A door from the other end of the room opened and 3 men trooped in carrying large steel bowls with lids on. These were set down on the tables and the men lifted the lids before joining the diners. The Marinos politely waited in turn to put their hands into the bowl and bring out a handful of eels and snails, which they put on their plate. Only this meal was not staying on the plate.

Bruno and Hamish watched in astonishment as the eels slithered around on the plate and the snails tried to find a route over the slimy mass. Hamish tried to stifle a giggle and ended up having to put his fist in his mouth. The Marinos ate in silence, picking from the outside of the plate so that the ones just about to fall off were eaten first. They didn't seem to mind that the eels continued to wriggle in their mouths and sometimes one would be hanging out of a mouth whilst the mouth's owner would be chewing the other end inside. The snail was a bit more work. As if breaking the shell of an egg, the snails were gently knocked against the edge of the table and any bits left on the snail flesh were picked off before the whole thing would be eaten in one gulp.

The door to the kitchen opened again, and a man carrying a tray walked up to the boys. Bruno closed his eyes momentarily expecting a writhing mass of food. To his relief, he was presented with some delicious looking prawns on a bed of something green. He looked intently at the prawns in case of any movement. There was none. Bruno looked at Hamish and grinned. They were both starving.

A man sitting opposite Finn spoke. He had eaten quickly and was now finished. He addressed Polperro. 'Do the boys know about us yet'?

'Not the whole story,' answered Polperro, looking at Bruno. 'I feel we need to introduce them to our world slowly. After all, it is a very unusual one. So Bruno, what do you think of Marino.'

Bruno quickened his chewing and swallowed. ' Well Sir, I think its fantastic. I still can't really believe that we're here, and I don't understand why you have decided to show us your secret place.'

Polperro sighed. 'We need help from Leylanders, and we felt it would be easier to talk to children rather than adults. We feel that you will understand us better, and are unlikely to tell others about us.'

'But what happens if we do?' asked Bruno nervously, wondering how he was going to keep **all this** a secret.

'Well, you didn't believe us until we brought you here. So why should anyone else? Your friends will assume you're making it up to impress them and your parents will think its just a game you've invented.' Bruno nodded. Polperro was right. His Aunt would just laugh, and his school friends would probably think it was some sort of a trick.

'What do you want from us anyway?' Hamish asked cheerfully as his gaze was caught by an eel wriggling from the mouth of one of the boys opposite.

'All in good time, my dears,' answered Polperro. 'This is a serious matter, and I don't want you to consider helping us until you've got to know a bit about our way of life. You mentioned you had to be home by 4. It's time to go back now.'

Finn stood up and went to get the boys wetsuits, which were now dry. The Marinos started to get up from the table and leave the room.

Hamish and Bruno pulled their wetsuits over their swimming trunks and made their way towards the large hole at the end of the room where they had come in. Pluto appeared from nowhere and nuzzled up to Hamish's foot. He picked him up and stroked him before unzipping his wet suit and pushing him inside.

Finn explained that Osquirt and Botolph were waiting for them outside the house and would return them to the cave. If they needed any help getting the boat back to the beach, the dolphins would help.

Finn looked at the boys. 'So, would you be able to come back again tomorrow? I can give you directions to get to the cave so that you don't have to borrow your aunt's boat and it will be much quicker for you to get out here again.'

Hamish stepped forward. 'Well, as long as you're going to tell us what is going on tomorrow, then I'm happy to come,' he nodded seriously, and looked at Bruno. Deep down, there was no way he wasn't going to come back but he sensed he ought to behave more responsibly for Bruno's sake. After all, he was the eldest.

'Yes, that's fine by me too,' said Bruno, a little too quickly.

'Okay, I promise,' said Finn. Polperro will tell you the whole story. Shall I meet you at the cave at 10.00ish.'

The boys nodded and climbed into their aquadaptor boots and down into the large hole hanging on to the bars. Finn came with them but had said that he would leave them once they had met up with the dolphins. A glass hatch slid across the top of the hole above them and the roaring noise they had heard before started up. Bruno looked at Hamish. Up till now he had been excited, but now felt a bit anxious about being plunged into deep water again without testing his aquadaptor boots. The water had reached his waist and he looked at Finn, his nervousness showing. Finn turned to the wall and lifted a lever. The water level stopped rising.

'You okay, Bruno?' Finn asked.

'Yeh, er no. Is there a chance that my boots won't work,' he asked shyly.

Finn laughed. 'No, but let's go slowly. I'll fill the chamber up to our chests, then we can duck down and get used to breathing underwater before I fill the rest of the chamber.' Bruno nodded. He was grateful that Finn understood and hadn't made him feel like a sissy. Hamish said nothing but it was clear from his expression that he hadn't been happy about the situation either. The chamber fill went smoothly. The boys ducked down and again experienced to their delight the experience of breathing without aid. They swam around in the chamber until the bottom hatch opened and they were able to follow Finn out. Osquirt and Botolph were swimming around outside the house and came alongside the boys who took hold of their dorsal fins in the same way as they had on their journey there. They waved to Finn and the dolphins set off. Bruno started to relax. This was so fantastic he couldn't believe it was happening. Riding a dolphin was something he had always dreamed about but had never imagined it would ever happen. He looked around and saw a large ray gracefully swimming past. Its enormous wings moving slowly to power it along. He waved at Hamish who grinned and waved back. All too soon, the dolphins arrived at the cave. The boys let go and swam in over the shallow shelf. They climbed out onto the ledge and were relieved to find Wishful moored up safely. Bruno took both pairs of Aquadaptors and followed Finn's instructions. He had explained there was a second ledge running along the back of the cave. At the far end of the ledge to the seaward side there was a loose rock on top of the ledge. Bruno lifted this off the ledge and found a large hole beneath, where he was to hide the Aquadaptors until tomorrow.

'Come on, better get going.' Bruno shouted to Hamish who had disappeared around a corner in the rock.

'Coming, I was just looking for the path that will bring us down from the cliff top. Finn said it should bring us out into the cave.'

'We haven't got time to look now. Let's leave it until tomorrow. I'm undoing the painter.' Bruno now wanted to get home; to a place he felt was safe and think about the days events. He was already trying to think of a story to tell Auntie Moo, but his mind seemed completely empty of anything apart from the truth, and he certainly couldn't say anything about Marino.

Hamish leapt into the boat and pushed off. He reached for one of the oars and started moving Wishful to the mouth of the cave. Finn had suggested that one of them lean out over the bow of the boat before coming out of the cave, as it would look odd if one minute there was no one there and the next this dinghy pops up from nowhere. There was a gentle breeze and Hamish hoisted the mainsail and unfurled the jib. Osquirt and Botolph were circling around and Bruno shouted. 'We're fine, we'll see you tomorrow, and waved at the dolphins.'

Bruno pulled in the sails and the little boat started to move forwards. There was no one else in sight, and they followed the cliffs until the beach came into view. Hamish pulled out the bag of sandwiches and handed one to Bruno. It was 3 o'clock. Plenty of time to get back to the house.

'I'm not sure that I can keep all this a secret.' Bruno took his eyes off the sail and looked at Hamish. He nodded as he chewed his sandwich. 'Hmm, except that Polperro is right. No one will believe us. Especially if we tell them about the lunch.' Hamish giggled.

'Auntie Moo might, she's a bit crazy,' added Bruno, taking a bite of his sandwich.

'Yes, but then she'll tell Uncle John,' answered Hamish. 'I think it's best if we keep it a secret.'

'OK, but don't blame me if it comes out by mistake,' said Bruno. 'Sometimes I get my words confused if people ask me the wrong questions.'

'Don't be silly Bruno,' Hamish said firmly. 'There's nothing to worry about. We're not doing anything wrong! It is completely weird but its also an adventure and we've been jolly lucky to be involved in it.' They were coming into the beach and Bruno was concentrating on turning Wishful into the wind and getting ready to pull the rudder up.

'Up centreboard,' called Bruno. Hamish obediently pulled up the little board that keeps Wishful moving in a straight line, and both boys jumped over the side into the shallow water, holding the front of the boat head on into the wind as they did so. Hamish ran up the beach for the trailer as Bruno let down the mainsail and furled the jib. Within minutes Wishful was safely back on her trailer and secured against the sea wall. The boys hastily pulled the blue canvas cover over the deck and tied it underneath. Auntie Moo had suggested they leave the sails and boom on the boat for the moment as they might go out again during the holiday.

'Where shall we say we've been?' asked Bruno anxiously.

'Just out for a sail,' Hamish answered with a touch of irritation in his voice. 'We've only been away for 5 hours!' Pluto was perched on his shoulder and Hamish stroked him affectionately. 'Unless you want to say we were kidnapped by mermaids.' He added wickedly. Bruno didn't find it funny.

'Look.' added Hamish grinning. 'We're having a problem ourselves. Believing what has just happened to us, so Polperro is right. They certainly won't believe us.'

The boys ran up the sandy path and turned right through the gate into the large garden. They raced up the lawn and into the kitchen through the back door. The kitchen was empty. Bruno relaxed. 'They're not back yet. Let's see what's in the fridge.

CHAPTER 5 – Paisley meets Osquirt

The following day was Saturday, and Auntie Moo, Paisley and Uncle John were already eating breakfast when the boys came down. Bosun, the Horror Pet was sitting on Bruno's chair and hissed when he tried to push him off. Auntie Moo stood up and gently picked up the hissing animal and put him down on the floor.

'I thought we'd all go out for a picnic today. Perhaps drive out to one of the other bays that you haven't seen yet.' She said as Bosun's hiss turned into a growl.

The boys looked at each other. A look of panic crept across Bruno's face.

Hamish spoke up. 'Er, we've arranged to meet a boy on the beach. We met him a few days ago. He knows all the good fishing places.'

'Oh, can I come?' Paisley had just finished her cereal, and was desperate to get down from the table before anyone spotted that she wasn't going to eat the half slice of buttered toast that Auntie Moo had prepared. She had already found out that unlike Raffi, their Cairn Terrier at home, Bosun didn't like toast, and dropping pieces under the table resulted in Auntie Moo giving her – Paisley, a dustpan and brush to clear the crumbs up.

Uncle John answered. 'Do you think your

new friend would like to come with us. There's plenty of room in the car, and you could arrange to go fishing with him another day.'

'It's not as easy as that,' said Bruno quickly. 'We really need to go fishing today.'

Auntie Moo looked at him and frowned. 'Why, what's so important about today?'

Hamish interrupted. 'Oh, its just that he's not going to be here for long, but it doesn't matter Bruno, we can go fishing tomorrow.' His eyes focussed on Bruno's and he gave a little nod to persuade Bruno to agree.

'That's settled then. After breakfast, you go and get your friend, and we'll get the picnic ready,' said Auntie Moo.

'Paisley, do you want to go with the boys?'

Paisley whispered, 'Yes.'

'Well, eat up your toast then.' Auntie Moo added kindly.

The boys left the house and walked down the garden in silence. Paisley was trailing behind. Once out on the beach path, Bruno whispered. 'It's far too early to go to the cave. It's only 9.00 o clock and anyway we can't take Paisley.'

'I know,' answered Hamish.' I think we should go down to the beach for a while and then tell Paisley that he's obviously not going to show up. I could then offer to go and look for him and leave a message in the cave. If I can find it. You're much better than me at that sort of thing. Perhaps you should go?'

'Except that Paisley will want to come with me,' answered Bruno glumly.

They had reached the corner of the beach. It was a hot day, and the sea looked like glass with only a few ripples coming into the bay.

'What does your friend look like?' asked Paisley looking out across the beach. She had her hand cupped over her eyes to shield them from the early sun and had pushed her long, blond hair away from her face, as she looked out to sea. She was standing on tiptoes as if to get a better view. Two families had started to put up windbreaks and deck chairs, and Paisley could see some cars pulling into the car park on the headland. Otherwise it was quite empty.

' He's got dark hair and is like us really,' answered Hamish looking around... 'apart from the fact that he's half a fish,' he added quietly under his breath.

Paisley turned round as a smile came to her face. 'What? What did you say?'

'Nothing.' Hamish laughed. 'Just teasing. We're probably too early for him, anyway. Let's leave it. We can meet up with him tomorrow.'

Bruno nodded, grateful for an answer to the problem. They'd think of something tomorrow. The three ran back to the house.

'Won't he be looking for you though?' asked Uncle John. 'I mean, perhaps we should wait till 10 o clock?'

'Oh no, its not that important, we'll see him tomorrow.' answered Hamish hurriedly. He wanted to get off the subject as Bruno was becoming agitated and might say something he didn't mean to.

Marlyn Bay is the next bay down to the East, and has many more rock pools than Lazy Haze beach. Paisley loved it. She insisted that her brother stay with her to help her catch fish and crabs from the pools, as she needed someone to hold the bucket. Bruno was relaxing into the day. He was absorbed with the fishing and had forgotten about yesterday's adventure for the moment. Hamish had disappeared over the top of the outbreak of rocks where Bruno and Paisley were fishing.

Bruno heard his name. He looked round to see Hamish standing on the top of the rocks pointing out to sea. 'Dolphins!'

Bruno and Paisley dropped their buckets and nets and scrambled up to join Hamish.

Following the line of his arm, they could see the fins of two dolphins quite close in. They were moving slowly and appeared to be waiting.

'Osquirt and Botolph,' murmured Bruno under his breath. 'Come on, let's swim out.'

Bruno ran back to where his Aunt and Uncle were sitting on the beach having made themselves what looked like a fairly permanent camp. There was a tent, a windbreak, 2 collapsible chairs, a waterproof mat covered in towels, and a large basket overflowing with cutlery, plates and Tupperware containers. They were both sitting in their chairs reading their newspapers.

'We're all going swimming.' Bruno cried. 'We won't be long.' He turned and started running towards the others before any reply could be given, but heard his Aunt shout back. 'Look after Paisley.' Bruno raised his arm to acknowledge that he'd heard, but didn't look back.

By the time he got back to the others they were already wading through the small surf breaking on the edge of the beach. Bruno ran in and dived through the waves, breaking into a fast crawl. He shouted at Hamish to stay with Paisley and sped on to where he had seen the dolphins. Bruno was sure it was Osquirt and Botolph and felt that he could make them take a message back to Finn if he could get to them. He stopped swimming and looked around. The fins were very close now and suddenly there was a splash from behind him.

'There you are. What happened?' It was Finn.

'Sorry, we couldn't get a message to you. My sister is with us, and my Aunt and Uncle wanted us to go with them for a picnic. They invited you too.'

'I guessed there was a problem.' Finn replied. 'Osquirt suddenly changed direction as we were on our way back to Marino from the cave. Dolphins are very clever and he obviously sensed you were here. Do you want to come and say hello to them?' asked Finn.

'I'd love to, but my sister is just behind us and she doesn't know anything about this,' answered Bruno.

'Don't worry, I'll disappear and send in Osquirt on his own. You can just pretend you've found a tame dolphin. Maybe see you tomorrow?'

'We'll be there,' smiled Bruno. Excited at the thought of being close to the dolphin again.

Finn dived and Bruno turned and waved to Hamish and Paisley who were slowly making their way towards him. At the same time, Bruno noticed Osquirt move in closer towards him. The dolphin came right up to Bruno and let him touch his nose. Osquirt then rolled over and made a chattering noise with his teeth. He was laughing, Bruno thought.

Paisley was quite out of breath when she arrived, and Bruno held her for a moment while treading water. 'You'll never believe what I've found Paisley. A tame dolphin, look.'

Hamish noticed that Bruno switched to baby language when he talked to his sister. It was a bit irritating, but then Hamish's sisters were older than him so he didn't have the same feelings towards them.

Osquirt swam up to Paisley and turned so that she could hold his dorsal fin. Paisley clung to Bruno with a mixture of fright and excitement. She slowly put out her hand to run it down the side of the animal's body.

'Its all slimy!' she shouted delightedly.

'Of course,' answered Hamish laughing. 'He's a big fish.

Osquirt started to move, accelerating fast away from them. He jumped out of the water landing with a big splash and came racing back towards them.

'Oh, I've never seen a dolphin before!' Paisley let go of Bruno and swam over to the dolphin. As if realising that she was a bit nervous, Osquirt gently moved himself so that her hand was resting over his fin, and then slowly started towing her towards the beach.

'He's taking her back to the beach,' cried Bruno. 'Come on.' The boys swam alongside Paisley who was speechless with delight. A large grin on her face.

As Osquirt entered the shallows he stopped and turned away from Paisley forcing her to let go. The dolphin moved slowly away from the group and was gone. Paisley couldn't control her excitement. She ran up the beach screaming at Auntie Moo. 'I've had a ride on a dolphin, I've had a ride on a dolphin.'

CHAPTER 6 – A surprisingly unusual story

The boys got up earlier than usual on Sunday. They needed to leave the house by 9.30 to have time to find the hidden tunnel down to the cave.

Polperro had been right about grown ups. They hadn't believed Paisley's story about the dolphin ride and whilst Bruno hadn't wanted to confirm Paisley's story, he was sorry that she had become so upset and frustrated when they wouldn't believe her.

'Shall we tell Paisley the truth,' asked Bruno as he was pulling on his T-shirt.

'There's no point, at the moment. Unless she is coming with us to visit Marino. Let's just wait and see what happens today,' answered Hamish sensibly. He felt that he already had one tell-tale on his hands, and he didn't want another.

Auntie Moo had packed them a sandwich lunch and wished them good luck with their fishing. Paisley had asked to go with them, but Hamish had pointed out that she'd be very bored and Bruno promised she could spend the next day with them, which seemed to satisfy her.

The boys set off with their fishing rods and back packs agreeing to be back by 4 o'clock.

Finn had explained that the entrance to the

secret tunnel was just off the cliff walk. Instead of turning left out of the garden gate towards the beach, the boys turned right and followed the path down towards the edge of the cliff. The path turned to the right before the edge and followed the line of the cliff. There was gorse on either side and no sign of the large heap of rocks that Finn had mentioned. The path continued on over a small hill with the edge of the cliff still close by on the left. Just over the brow of the hill, the boys could see a mass of rocks on the right hand side just as Finn had described. They quickened their pace and Hamish looked behind him to make sure there was no one else in sight.

Finn had explained that at the back of the rock mass, one of the rocks looked like a mushroom. On top of the mushroom rock there was another small one. The boys had to stand on this small rock, which would press it into the larger one, and a door would open.

They looked at each other as they arrived at the mushroom shaped rock. Bruno jumped up onto it and put his right foot onto the smaller one that seemed to be balancing on top. Nothing happened.

'Put all your weight on it, ' Hamish cried.

Bruno lifted his other leg and balanced on the small rock. A movement came from

Hamish's left and they both turned to see what had been a mossy slope move sideways to reveal a tunnel.

The boys had to bend over to get through the entrance but once inside, the roof opened up and they were able to stand up. Bruno stood on another rock just inside the opening as Finn had instructed, and the opening closed behind them. There were lines of light coming into the tunnel through the rocks above, and the boys were able to see enough to follow the tunnel until they reached the cave. They had to jump down a series of ledges that formed big steps to arrive at the waterside ledge where they were to meet Finn. He was waiting.

Bruno and Hamish sat patiently in the Breathable Room while Finn went off to get Polperro. The dolphin ride had been even more enjoyable than the first time as the boys were more relaxed and knew where they were going. Pluto stayed in Hamish's swimming trunk pocket and only came out once they arrived in the Breathable Room when he went off to find his new crab friends.

Polperro was wearing a robe made out of more seaweed material. This and his white beard made him look like a great sea lord and Bruno and Hamish stood up quickly when he came into the room.

Polperro raised his arms in welcome. 'Hello my young friends, did you find us easily today?' The boys nodded and Polperro waved his arms suggesting they sit down again.

'Well, I'm going to tell you a story. It will be a true story, but it won't sound like one. Just try and believe me, if you can.' He looked at the boys. Hamish had his head on his chin leaning on the table and Bruno sat with his hands in his lap. They both looked at Polperro eager to hear more.

'Hundreds of years ago, Cornwall was well known for its wrecking and smuggling. Some say the Cornish would light fires on the land, pretending to be lights in a port. This would mislead the sailing captains into thinking it was safe to approach. The ships would then be sent crashing onto the rocks nearby. I don't know whether these stories are true, but there were many wrecks off the Cornish coast years ago. What is true is that the Cornish people believed that the cargo from these wrecked ships was theirs by right, and some were ruthless in claiming it.

Around 1860, a young woman was on the ship "Carcasson" sailing from Bristol to Africa. She was going out there to start a new life with her husband. She was pregnant with their first child. They were caught in a terrible storm and it is believed the smugglers lured the ship onto the rocks out here near Oldquay. The ship went down, there were 78 lives lost. The captain and one of his crew survived. The captain claims that the young woman went into labour as the ship went down, and he is haunted by her cries.'

'A couple of years later, a young doctor and his wife were walking on Lazy Haze beach and found a child playing by the rocks. He was naked, and his hair was so long it had obviously never been cut. They took him home and asked around the neighbourhood to try and find his identity. Nobody came forward and they decided to bring the boy up as their own. One year, in the summer, the family was on the beach paddling, and the young child ran into the water. He fell over and his father panicked and ran in after him. When he got to the child, he saw that the boy was fine. He was swimming and the doctor realised that he could breath underwater. He picked the boy up and took him home saying nothing to his wife. As a doctor he now knew his son was different to normal boys. There were no x-ray machines at that time so he gave his son a thorough examination. He found 2 flaps of skin on his left side above his waist as you have seen on Finn.

So this is the story of our ancestors. Any child born to a Marino man will always have ½ gills ½ lungs.

During the First World War, life was very difficult for people here. Some of our people went to war, but the rest of the Marinos who stayed here in Cornwall had a bad time. There was no food, no money, no proper home. Our ancestors decided to return to the sea. They built this house with their own hands, using rocks from the seabed. They used the steel from containers that had fallen off ships to strengthen the house, and they lived on fish and shellfish. In those days there was no power down here, and none of these rooms had air in them. Marinos married to Leylanders would spend some of their time here and some of their time on land with their wives or husbands. It wasn't ideal. But then a wind farm was built nearby. We were able to connect up to this secretly and get electricity. It has meant we are able to heat our home, our water, cook, and to pump oxygen into this house. The Leylanders don't miss it as it is such a tiny amount and anyway if something goes wrong at the farm, we swim over and sort it out for them before they've noticed, so saving them time and money.'

Bruno had heard of wind farms. His class were doing a project on them at school and he had been fascinated to learn that these enormous windmills were able to produce electricity from the wind.

Polperro continued. 'This is why we need your help. This windfarm has been running for 20 years now and a new Windfarm Development company want to take it down and replace it with newer turbines. They want to move the whole thing much further out to sea where they can put 250 turbines up as opposed to the 30 they have here. You can see it will give us a big problem if this happens. It will mean we will have to move our home.'

Hamish nodded. He could see that the house must have taken ages to build and they seemed to have everything really well organised in the house. Much better than Auntie Moo's house or his own parents. This house had lots of exciting gadgets which made it much more fun.

'But what can we do to help?' asked Bruno with a frown on his face.

'We need information from the Windfarm Developers,' Polperro replied.' We can't go to them direct as we don't want to draw attention to ourselves and we don't have an address for them to reply to. They are holding public meetings at the village hall in Oldquay, and we wondered whether you could go to one of these meetings and find out their plans. We don't know what we can do about all this but it may be that we can get them to change their minds somehow.'

'But what kind of information would help,' asked Bruno, eager to help his new friends.

Polperro placed his hands on Bruno's shoulders. 'I don't know Bruno, but we can't do nothing and let them take away our home. Once we have some information about their plans, maybe we'll think of something. If not, then we'll simply go back to the way we used to live and our Leylander people will have to move back to the mainland until we have sorted a new power system out. Anyway, do you think you would be able to help us?'

Hamish stood up. 'Yes.' He looked at Bruno. 'We are doing a project on windfarms at school, and we can ask Auntie Moo if we can go to one of the talks.' 'That would be easy.' Bruno beamed.

Polperro laughed. 'Good, that's settled. I'll give you a list of questions before you go. Now, if you both have time, we are having a 'Blue' afternoon this afternoon. This is when we have games for the children outside the house in what we call the 'Big Blue.' Finn can include you into the teams if you want.' The boys' faces lit up. It sounded exciting. 'Great,' said Bruno. 'We don't have to leave till 3.00.'

CHAPTER 7 – Dolphin Rush

Game No. 1 was called 'The Dolphin Rush,' with Osquirt and Botolph and 6 other members of their family producing the dolphin power. Bruno and Hamish were introduced to their team members in the 'Breathable Room.' Argot was a small, thin boy whose jet-black hair was down to his shoulders. He had never been out of Marino and had grown up completely unaware of normal life on the Mainland. His mother was a traditional Gillander spending most of her time at Marino, and she couldn't see the point of her son leaving the sea house until he was grown up. Finn introduced him as a demon player in the 'Dolphin Rush.'

One of the team leaders was a girl called Coral, who was slightly taller than Bruno with dark hair, which was cut short. She was an excellent swimmer and because her parents allowed her to go to the mainland, she had much more confidence than Argot. She chatted easily to the boys.

'And this is my best friend Nemone,' she said as she pulled her friend forward towards Bruno. Nemone had the bluest eyes that Bruno had ever seen. With her long dark hair, Bruno thought her to be even prettier than his sister Paisley, who he had always thought was the best looking girl he knew.

'How do you do?' Bruno held out his hand.

'Fine, thank you,' Nemone answered shyly. 'Are you the boys that are going to help us to save our home?'

Hamish stepped forward. 'We're going to try.' He held out his hand to Nemone in the hope that she might give him the same smile that she had given Bruno.

There were more players. An older boy called Fluke who had no hair on his deep brown head, and a small, thin girl called Brill, who looked younger than the rest of them.

Coral interrupted.' Shall I explain the rules of the game.' She sat down on the floor cross-legged. She was wearing an ordinary swimming costume. It was orange with brown flowers, which matched her deep tan. Hamish decided that she was a bit of a tomboy and likely to be tougher and faster underwater than the other girls. He hoped he would be on her team.

'Each of us rides a dolphin and there is a sort of a pitch,' she started to explain, 'which is a large valley area between two coral reefs. Each of these reefs has a small net basket sitting on top of it. They are made of seaweed with an open top. We don't use a ball, but a small fish called a puffa fish. He agrees to be used for the game on the condition that we catch his dinner for the next week.' Coral paused and looked at the boys. 'He has a very prickly skin so it is difficult to hold him too hard, and the more exciting the game becomes you find you tighten your hand on him and he will puff out more and get more prickly. We position ourselves a bit like a football team on the pitch. The idea is to get the fish into the net and score a puff. You can tackle the other team by taking the fish out of their hand. It is not difficult because you can't hold the puffa fish tightly and we often drop the puffa anyway. The most important thing is to hang on to your own dolphin. If you fall off, your team will be given a penalty of 2 points. Any questions?'

Finn took team leader position and chose Bruno, Fluke and Nemone to be on his side, and Coral was nominated as the other team leader heading up a team with Argo, Hamish and Brill. Finn and Coral picked a piece of seaweed off the sea floor. The person who picked the longest won and took the first puffa. Bruno was sitting astride Osquirt and Hamish was on Botolph. Because these were the fastest dolphins of the group, Finn decided the boys would be safer on them. Faster to get out of danger if anyone was likely to be hurt, he said, although Bruno couldn't see what the danger might be. He didn't have long to wait.

Finn picked the longest piece of seaweed, picked up the puffa fish and was off. His dolphin spurted forward towards the ledge only to be blocked by Coral on her dolphin. Finn let go the puffa and his No. 2, Fluke, smoothly grabbed the fish and went on towards the ledge. Botolph knew the game well, and suddenly Hamish was holding on as tightly as he could. Botolphs's whole body now moving quickly to get to Fluke, but as they got close, Fluke saw them, and he and his dolphin curled upwards and went straight for the surface. Hamish saw them breaking through into the sunlight and then disappear. Coral was after them, and within seconds, Fluke reappeared, but now much closer to the ledge. Botolph and Hamish were already there. They blocked the way and Coral snatched the puffa out of Fluke's hand. Coral and her dolphin sped across the sea pitch, dodging Finn and arriving at the ledge where she dropped the puffa in the basket. She turned and smiled and held up one finger to Bruno who had followed in close pursuit.

It was Coral's turn to start and within minutes she had passed the puffa to Argot having been tackled by Finn. Whilst Argot was small, he was wiry and strong, and his dolphin knew he would hold on whatever twisting manoeuvres had to be made. Fluke approached, but Argot and his dolphin dived, and the dolphin rolled over onto his back so that Argot was now upside down on the dolphin's back and the two of them swam straight under Fluke. They then shot to the surface. Finn pursued them and Bruno saw Finn grab the puffa out of Argot's hand. Suddenly Hamish appeared on Botolph and blocked Finn's way. He released the puffa from his hand as he passed close to Nemone hoping she would be able to take up the chase, but she held back nervously and was pushed out the way by Fluke who grabbed it just as the fish was about to drop down into the sand. He and his dolphin picked up speed and raced across the pitch to deliver the puffa into the basket. One all.

As the teams were re-organising themselves back into their start positions, Bruno heard a rumbling noise above. Everybody stopped moving, and the dolphins all turned towards the direction of the noise. Finn let go his dolphin, and swam towards the noise. He disappeared out of sight. Hamish and Bruno looked at each other and shrugged their shoulders. When Finn appeared all the dolphins moved towards him and he beckoned the group to follow.

Not far ahead there was an enormous wall of fish netting, which was moving slowly to the left. It looked to Bruno as if it was held up at the top by something invisible, which was just below the water. He later learned it was held up by a row of small buoys that sat just below the water's surface. The net was teaming with fish of all sizes that had tried to swim through the net and had got stuck. Bruno turned towards Hamish who looked horrified. Finn motioned as if to go back and he led the way towards Marino.

Polperro was waiting for them all in the Breathable Room and Finn quickly told him about the net. Whilst there was nothing illegal in that kind of fishing, Polperro was always concerned that the net might get caught on something nearby and then divers would be sent down. They would be sure to find the house, as it was so big.

Polperro listened intently to Finn. His serious face looking earnestly at the boy as he took in all that Finn had to say. They spoke in low voices and Bruno watched as Finn left the room, returning shortly afterwards with a young man. Polperro turned to Bruno and Hamish, 'Boys, this is Penpol, my no. 2 here. He helps me with running the house and looks after some of our fishing interests. Penpol, could you gather together some of our people to go and keep an eye on the net. Release as many of the fish as possible and if the net gets tangled in any way, please cut it so that it can drift away.' Penpol nodded, smiled at the boys and left the room.

Polperro turned to the boys and explained. 'We don't want any divers coming down here to untangle fishing nets, you see, or all could be revealed.'

The hubbub in the room was increasing as the Dolphin Rush team started talking excitedly about the game. Polperro laughed and waved the children away. 'Bruno, I have a list here of the sort of questions we need answering. It has been printed on paper and sealed in plastic so the ink will not run. We have a dry water taxi system if you would prefer to use that today although it will take you to Oldquay and not back to the cave.'

'That would be cool,' exclaimed Hamish excitedly. Everything about this world appealed to him, and he was sure the dry water taxi was going to be just as unusual as everything else.

Bruno looked at Hamish shaking his head. 'We've left our fishing rods at the cave. We will have to go there anyway to pick them up. Perhaps we can use the water taxi next time.'

'No problem, no problem, I just want you to see all the elements of our world down here, but another time,' said Polperro gently. 'It is time

63

for you to go.

Finn, please arrange to meet the boys in Oldquay in a few days time so they might visit us again in the water taxi.' Polperro got up to say goodbye.

CHAPTER 8 – Bosun's supper

It was supper time at Magellan House and everyone was busily tucking into the homemade pasta dish that Auntie Moo had prepared.

'So what have you been up to?' asked Uncle John.

'Well, we've done a bit of fishing but didn't catch anything,' Hamish answered, aware that Bruno was looking at him nervously.

'I hope you're going to take Paisley with you tomorrow. She needs a day with people her own age,' said Auntie Moo.

Bruno nodded at her and then looked at Paisley who was looking up at him with one of her *I adore my brother* looks. 'Okay, what would you like to do tomorrow Paisley.'

By now, Paisley had got a mouthful of pasta in her mouth, but managed to speak at the same time. 'Erm, go sailing?' she said quickly, but firmly.

'Well, that depends on the weather,' answered Auntie Moo. Also the tide is not helpful as it is low water this afternoon which means you'll have an awfully long walk with the dinghy back from the water's edge, but I suppose I could help you.'

'I was wondering if we could sail out and around the windfarm. Its not that far, is it?' said

Hamish.

'Its possible if the wind isn't too strong,' answered Auntie Moo, 'and it would be a good direction to go towards the windfarm anyway as the tide will be against you on the way out and with you on the way back.'

'Good that's settled then,' exclaimed Bruno with too much enthusiasm. He realised this was a good excuse to get into a conversation about windfarms.

'Uncle John, We're doing a project on windfarms at school. Do you know if we can get any information on the one here.'

Uncle John frowned. 'Well, I'm afraid there is talk of the windfarm developers pulling this one down. They want to build a much larger one further out to sea which the locals aren't very happy about, and I am even less happy.'

'Why?' asked Hamish. 'If it's further out, then no one will see it.'

'Well, from the airport's point of view, it is likely to interfere with our radar system, in which case it will be a real problem.'

'And as far as the view is concerned, it won't be that far out,' Auntie Moo interrupted. 'You'll see it on most fine days, and the locals are unhappy about the noise and mess all the lorries make in the town whilst they are building it. There is an open meeting about it all tomorrow night at the local village hall, but I can't really believe you'd be interested in coming.'

'We would,' cried Bruno and Hamish together. Auntie Moo and Uncle John looked at the boys. 'Well, I am surprised,' said Uncle John. 'Then let's all go along and see what's happening.'

Paisley woke the boys early. She was dressed in shorts and a tee shirt and already had her life jacket on over the top. 'Come on sleepy heads, if you don't get up, I'll let Bosun in.'

Bosun had a nasty habit of jumping on beds and finding a warm body to lie on top of. Ideally very close to your face, so that with one paw he could flick your cheek to try and make you wake up and stroke him. This would continue until you gave in.

Bruno wasn't in the mood for Bosun this morning. He slowly got out of bed. 'Thanks Paisley. Why don't you go downstairs and put some toast on. Also see if there is anything in the fridge that we can make a picnic with.' He loved his sister dearly but sometimes she was really irritating and at these times he decided that the bossy big brother approach was the best.

Auntie Moo was already in the kitchen

making a picnic. 'Would you like some ham today Paisley,' she asked.

'I only eat salami and cucumber,' answered Paisley coyly.

'I know that's your favourite, but I thought you might like a change.' She looked at Paisley who by now had tears welling up in her eyes.

'No problem, salami and cucumber, it is,' finished Auntie Moo.

Bosun was curled up on the kitchen chair and Paisley went to give him a stroke. He rolled over on his back and forgetting he was on a chair, started to slide off the side. He quickly turned so that he landed on the floor on his feet, hissed at Paisley, and disappeared under the kitchen table.

'Do you think Bosun would like to come sailing with us, Auntie Moo?'

'Well, I don't think so. He can't swim and would be frightened. Cats don't like the water.

'Well, that's a bit odd,' said Paisley seriously, 'as his favourite food is fish!'

Auntie Moo laughed. 'You're quite right Paisley. I had never thought of it like that.'

The boys arrived in the kitchen and sat down at the breakfast table. Pluto who had been up till now quite happy to spend most of his day in Hamish's pocket decided to poke his head out. Unfortunately, Bosun was still sitting quietly under the table cleaning his paws, and was amazed to see this extraordinary creature appear from Hamish's leg. It looked very tasty.

'Yeow,' screamed Hamish as he leapt to his feet. Bosun was hanging by his nails onto Hamish's shorts. Pluto had managed to jump over Bosun's head and was racing towards the living room door.

'Get him off me,' cried Hamish as Bosun tried to untangle his claws from the cotton shorts. Auntie Moo leapt up and grabbed the now wild animal. All but one of his claws had become free. The last one was still attached and Auntie Moo was trying to calm Hamish and Bosun down enough to be able to release it.

Once free Hamish rushed into the living room but Pluto was nowhere to be seen.

'Come on Bruno, we must find him before Bosun does,' said Hamish urgently. They disappeared out of sight.

'Oh dear. Bosun 's causing trouble again,' sighed Auntie Moo.

'It's not his fault,' said Paisley quietly. 'Pluto looks a bit like a big fish and Bosun likes fish.'

Uncle John laughed. 'Yes, but I doubt if Pluto tastes like fish. More like snake I should think. For all our sakes, I hope they find him.'

There was a shout from inside the house. Hamish appeared round the door carrying

Pluto. He was hiding in the upstairs loo.

'Its lucky we noticed him or else someone could have flushed him away by mistake,' Hamish said gravely.

'Well, I think that's enough animal drama for the day.' Auntie Moo smiled. 'I've made your picnic. When you come back in this afternoon, I suggest one of you boys comes and finds me and then I can give you a hand pulling her back up the beach.'

'Her, who is her?' said Paisley scornfully.

'Boats are always referred to as her,' answered Auntie Moo. They used to say it was because she needed painting up to make her look good similar to women wearing make up. Also they thought that it wasn't the initial expense of the boat that was costly but the looking after part, which men used to say about women. Of course, they wouldn't be allowed to say that now with equality and all that. I think the truth is that a good boat has beautiful lines and needs to be treated well. If you want the best from a boat, you need to be gentle and do things slowly.'

'See Paisley. So you have to do as you're told today and no messing about,' said Bruno forcefully.

Paisley nodded.

CHAPTER 9 – Paisley goes for a swim

There was a gentle wind from the South West. The Windfarm lay to the north east of the beach, which would mean that sailing out to the Windfarm, and back would be quite straightforward. The boys prepared the dinghy and pushed her to the water's edge. The tide was high and the three of them found it easy to launch her. Paisley and Bruno held her in the shallow water whilst Hamish walked the trailer back up the beach.

Paisley sat just behind the mast in the centre of the dinghy and Hamish sat on the side just behind her on the left hand side of the boat. Bruno climbed in over the back of the boat, and pulled the mainsail in, to get her moving through the surf. They were quickly clear of the shore and moved silently across the bay, out towards the Windfarm. The wind was blowing steadily and Hamish leant back and stretched his legs.

'What a day for a sail, the wind is just right.' He looked out towards the Windfarm and noticed a fin just in front of the dinghy. 'Look. Its Botolph,' he cried and dipped his hand over the side trying to make a noise with his fingers as he did so.

'Botolph, Botolph, who is that?' shouted

Paisley not able to contain her excitement at seeing the dolphin again. 'Oh, never mind Paisley, it's just a name we've given him.' Hamish muttered, now leaning right over the side.

'Be careful, Hamish, you're going to tip the boat,' cried Bruno.

At that moment, Paisley moved to the same side as the boys to get a better view, the overall weight of the three was too much for the gentle wind trying to balance the boat and Wishful lurched sideways. Hamish and Bruno managed to hold on but Paisley was catapulted from her seat into the water. The boat leaned right over, then tipped back the other way and came to a stop as she headed straight into the wind, her sails flapping.

'Paisley, where are you?' screamed Bruno, searching the water all around the boat in panic. 'Help!' cried Paisley in return. Her life jacket had brought her quickly to the surface, but she had swallowed a lot of water and was coughing uncontrollably. Bruno swung the boat round towards her and shouted at Hamish to take down the mainsail. At that moment, he heard another voice.

'Its okay, I'll get her.' It was Finn. He swam over to the now hysterical Paisley. She was sobbing uncontrollably and kept getting water in her mouth as each wave passed by. Finn approached her slowly. 'Paisley. I am Bruno's friend. Lie on your back and I will pull you back to the boat.' Paisley swam frantically towards Finn and put her arms around his neck. 'Okay.' Finn nodded smiling. 'That will do.' He held her head out of the water whilst kicking his feet and manouvered them both back to the boat. Bruno who was about to jump overboard hauled his sister back into the boat. She was still crying. Bruno put his arms round her.

'Its all right, you're fine now. Come on. Cheer up. Botolph and Osquirt are coming back to see you.' The two dolphins were now right beside the boat and Paisley put her hand out to touch Osquirt's nose. She felt better already. Finn had hauled himself into the boat and was keeping it steady whilst Paisley stroked the dolphins. He grinned. 'Well, Captain Bruno, where are you headed?'

'We thought we'd go out to see the Windfarm. Do you want to come with us?' answered Bruno.

'On the basis of the last couple of minutes, I think I'd better come to make sure you don't get into any more trouble,' said Finn, laughing.

Paisley smiled with delight… 'And the dolphins?'

'Yes,' Finn smiled as he looked at her.

'They'll come with us too, and if you like you can swim with them.'

'Yes, please.' Paisley squealed. In her excitement, she had forgotten that she didn't have a clue who Finn was, and how Bruno and Hamish knew him and the dolphins. She loved the dolphins already and couldn't wait to swim with them again.

'Hang on,' Bruno said with a frown on his face. 'Let's just get to the Windfarm and give Paisley a chance to calm down. We'll see what the wind is like out there, before she goes back into the water.'

Paisley nodded and Hamish pulled the mainsail back up the mast. The little boat gathered speed and Paisley took her position back in the centre of the boat. Osquirt and Botolph swam around the boat, charging underneath the boat's hull and then throwing themselves out of the water on the other side. Sometimes they would swim just in front of the boat as if trying to race.

Bruno steered the boat right up to one of the large wind turbines and found a metal ring at water level, which he tied the boat up to. They ate their lunch whilst Osquirt and Botolph played around the boat. At first they would shoot out squirts of water from their mouth into the boat, but because this didn't have much effect, they then brought clumps of seaweed from the seabed. By turning their heads quickly, they were able to throw the clumps hard into the boat usually hitting one of the sailors. A rather unpleasant experience, a bit like having a wet rag thrown at you.

Suddenly, Osquirt threw a small lobster, which came flying into the boat narrowly missing Finn who was sitting on that side. 'Ah, my lunch,' said Finn. He picked up the lobster and took a knife that was strapped to his side. He plunged the knife into the head of the lobster, until it stopped moving. Paisley shivered. Finn then cut the lobster down the middle and pulled the white flesh out of the body. He offered it around. Paisley who had watched all this in horror was speechless and shook her head. She took a mouthful of her salami and cucumber sandwich in silence.

'But its not cooked,' exclaimed Bruno.

'That doesn't matter. It tastes jolly good as it is,' answered Finn with a mouthful of lobster meat. Try it.'

Hamish gingerly took a tiny piece of the flesh and put it to his mouth having smelt it first. 'Hmm, its good, but I think it's nicer when it's cooked.' Finn laughed. 'So, is Paisley going to have a swim with Osquirt?'

'Oh, yes,' Paisley cried. 'Can I?'

Finn stood up in the boat. 'Osquirt, go and pick up 2 pairs of aquadaptors for our friends and bring them back to me as quickly as you can.'

'Um, Finn, is that a good idea? Paisley doesn't know anything about all this,' Bruno whispered.

'So tell her. Your Aunt and Uncle will never believe her. Believe me. I've told loads of children and no one **ever** believes them.' He said emphasising the ever.

Bruno and Hamish nodded. It was easy for Finn to say that but Bruno would have preferred to keep Paisley out of it. Auntie Moo would get very suspicious if Paisley went on enough about the dolphins. She was no ordinary Aunt.

Osquirt returned with the boots and Finn showed Paisley how they worked.

Bruno took off his life jacket and pulled on the aquadaptors. He then climbed carefully over the back of the boat so as not to overbalance the others. 'Come on Paisley, I'll be here with you all the time,' he said reassuringly. Paisley took off her lifejacket and followed Bruno in over the back of the boat.

'Hold onto the side first, and just dip your head underwater, open your mouth and take a breath,' he instructed.

Paisley looked at him glumly while treading water. 'I can't do that!'

'Of course you can. I'm here. Look, I'll show you.' Bruno dropped down below the surface but turned towards Paisley so that she could see his face. He opened his mouth and took a breath, pursing his lips to show her that he was breathing.

'I really just want to go swimming with Osquirt, I don't want to go underwater,' said Paisley. Bruno started to get impatient. 'Look, you're really lucky to be here with us today. Finn, Botolph and Osquirt are our secrets. If you don't want to go underwater, let's get back in the boat and go home.'

'Okay, Okay, I'm going under.' Paisley bent her head over so that she could see straight down to the seabed and took a breath. She held onto the side of the boat and seemed to be lying perfectly still. Bruno dived down and looked up at his little sister. She was lying now very still on the water and had let go of the boat. She had the biggest grin on her face that he had ever seen. He motioned her to dive down. She kicked her legs and was soon beside him. Osquirt appeared from nowhere and Botolph swam up beside Bruno. Paisley reached out and took Osquirt's dorsal fin and no sooner had she gripped her hand round it, Osquirt moved off.

Slowly at first, and then faster as he felt his passenger relax. Bruno grabbed Botolph and they soon caught up with Paisley and Osquirt, who by this time were diving down to the seabed and then turning and heading straight up to the surface only to change direction there and plummet quickly down to the seabed. Paisley loved it and pointed to a large crab running sideways across the sand. Osquirt slowed down so that Paisley could have a closer look. She let go of Osquirt and swam after the crab but he was too quick for her and disappeared under a ledge of coral. She turned to look for Osquirt again. Her long, blond hair moving as if in slow motion. Bruno was delighted with the way she took to the underwater world. Whilst she was very girlie about many things, she was also a bit of a tomboy and he felt proud of her. He pointed to the underneath of the boat, and they swam up to the surface.

'Amazing, amazing,' Paisley squealed. 'It's like magic.'

'Yes, and you're not to tell anyone about it. It's our secret. Is that clear?' said Bruno firmly. Paisley nodded. 'But can't we tell Auntie Moo, she can keep a secret.'

'No Paisley,' answered Bruno. 'She'd tell Uncle John and he wouldn't believe it and think we were up to something. Then we wouldn't be allowed to come out here anymore.'

They pulled themselves back into Wishful. Finn and Hamish were relaxing in the sunshine. Hamish looked at his watch. 'I think we ought to go Bruno, if we're to be back by 4.00.'

'Yes, you're right,' answered Bruno. 'But the wind seems to have dropped.'

'No problem,' cut in Finn. 'What do you call that rope at the front.'

'The painter,' answered Hamish quickly, proud to show his friends that he had learnt all the sailing terms this year.

'Is it long enough to tie a loop into it?' asked Finn. 'Botolph and Osquirt would be happy to tow you home.'

Bruno jumped forward onto the deck area in front of the mast and tied a large loop into the painter. He then dangled it over the front of the boat. Almost immediately Botolph took the hint and pushed his nose through the loop. 'Hold on,' Bruno shouted as he grabbed hold of the mast. 'We're off!'

Botolph and Osquirt took turns in the tow whilst the boys relaxed and Hamish explained to Finn that they would be going to the Windfarm meeting that evening. Paisley sat in her place behind the mast. Her head bent forward to catch sight of the dolphins who she now regarded as her best friends. As they neared the beach Finn took the Aquadaptors and jumped into the water, waving as he went. He didn't reappear and Bruno asked Hamish to raise the small jib, which would be enough to take them into the beach.

Chapter 10 – An enormous windfarm

The village hall was packed and Auntie Moo realised they had probably left it too late to get seats. There were two, right at the front and she suggested that the boys might like to take these whilst she and Uncle John would stand at the back. Bruno nodded, aware that they should be offering these seats to his uncle and aunt, but the thought of being so close would, he felt, help give him the nerve to stand up and ask questions.

In front of the seats facing them, there was a youngish man with very dark hair, wearing glasses. His assistant was a lady who was older than the man and was sorting out the electric leads for the projector.

He introduced himself. 'Welcome everyone, and thank you for finding time to come out tonight to hear about our exciting new windfarm development. My name is Peter Brewer and my assistant is Fiona.'

He pressed a button on the projector and talked through some slides explaining where the proposed windfarm was to be built, and showed an artist's illustration of how it might look from the shore. He talked about the number of houses that would be able to use the electricity generated by the windfarm and explained how the power would run in large cables under the seabed, to the shore. He then went on to talk about the timing of the project and explained how a bigger windfarm would be better for the area for various reasons. Neither Hamish nor Bruno could understand these reasons and they both looked at each other and shrugged their shoulders. They knew they didn't have to understand everything. They had been given the questions by Polperro and had memorised them over the previous few days. It was agreed that Bruno would ask two and Hamish would ask two.

'Any questions?' Peter turned to the audience as he finished talking. Bruno's hand shot up at the same time as a lady sitting 2 seats away from him. Peter looked at both of them and pointed to the lady.

'Yes,' Peter nodded towards her.

'Why do you need a new windfarm when there is already one here. If it is not big enough, why can't you just make it bigger?' The woman asked confidently.

'Good question. The seabed around the existing one here is pure, hard rock and it would be very difficult to pile down into it.' Bruno glanced at Uncle John before putting his hand up again. Peter nodded at him. Bruno stood up.

'We've heard that you will pull down the old

windfarm if the new one goes ahead. Can't you leave it as it is?' Bruno asked nervously.

'Ah,' Peter answered frowning. 'That's an interesting question. Where did you hear that from?'

Bruno started to stutter. 'Um, I can't remember, but I know someone said something about it.'

Uncle John's voice boomed out from the back of the hall. 'But it's true, isn't it? The old windfarm will be decommissioned if the new one goes ahead because it will affect the winds around the new one.'

'And you are?' asked Peter slowly.

'John Collins, Operations Director of Cornwall airport,' he smiled as he finished speaking.

'The old wind-farm will give us some problems, but we expect to be able to get round them,' Peter looked at Uncle John.

A hand went up at the back and Bruno sat down. His face had gone red and he was shaking, but at least they had two of the answers Polperro needed.

Peter was answering another question about noise and as soon as he had finished, Hamish put his hand up. Peter nodded at him.

'Is the place that you have chosen likely to change at all. I mean, what happens if the seabed is too hard there to build anything on?'

Peter smiled and answered the question although he did wonder why these kids needed to know such things.

'We have already done some tests on the seabed. Our next job will be to erect a test wind mast on the site next week. This will help us understand how difficult it will be to drill into the seabed and also give us an idea of wind strength and direction. Next.' He pointed to a lady sitting at the back of the hall.

Hamish nudged Bruno to remind him it was his turn. Bruno shook his head. He felt too embarrassed. Hamish put his hand up again.

'Hang on a minute, I'll come back to you once some other people have had a chance.' He nodded at Hamish as he spoke, and looked around the room choosing a young man who asked a question about the number of jobs the windfarm would provide. Peter continued to answer questions whilst Hamish and Bruno squirmed in their seats. Now both embarrassed and worried that they didn't have enough information for Polperro.

'OK, young man, what was it? This is the final question now.'

Hamish stood up 'Er, where exactly is the windfarm going to be built?' Peter looked at him, clearly irritated now. 'I showed you that on the slide earlier. Off Oldquay harbour and about 15 miles out to sea.'

'Oh yes, but where exactly. Do you know the latitude and longitude?' Hamish hoped that Peter wouldn't ask him what latitude and longitude meant as he hadn't got a clue, but it was something that Polperro was desperate to find out. Peter frowned.

'Look boys, can I just ask. What do you need all this information for?' he said in a slow and rather frightening way.

'Well, we are doing a project at school and we're trying to collect as much information as we can,' Hamish answered.

'Oh I see,' answered Peter relaxing. 'Well, we have just put up a new website. Oldquaywindfarm. You'll find lots of information on there.'

Hamish muttered thank you under his breath and sat down. He smiled at Bruno, who smiled back.

CHAPTER 11 – The Big Plan

Finn had explained that the tide taxi ran from the basement of one of the large hotels in Oldquay. The Headland Hotel was a large old building that looked like something out of a fairy tale. It was built on a crop of rocks sticking out into the bay from the town. A shaft had been drilled down the centre of the rocks and a lift fitted so that the hotel guests could get down to the hotel's private beach. Bruno and Hamish took a bus into town and walked out to the hotel. They had a towel and a bag with them to look as if they were guests at the hotel, and soon found the lift that had a big sign above it saying:

'To the Beach'

The hotel was very busy with families and children, but no one got into the lift with them. Finn had said that once at beach level, the main passage out to the beach was to the right, but to the left the passageway continued back into the cliff.

The boys turned left as they stepped out of the lift. There was no one around. A large board was propped up across the passage in front of them.

'NO   ADMITTANCE,   STRICTLY PRIVATE.'

Hamish looked at Bruno, who shrugged. They squeezed past the sign and walked down the dark passage. Finn had told them to take the second turning on the right and then the first on the left. At the end of this, they would come to a stone door. They simply had to pull it.

'Here it is, I'll open it,' whispered Hamish, looking excitedly at Bruno. He curled his fingers around the left hand side of the big stone and slowly pulled. The stone moved out towards him. The boys could see another passage beyond the stone and some light. They walked into the passage and the door closed behind them. Within a few steps, they arrived in a large underground cave which had a shaft of light pouring onto the water from above. The difference between this cave and the one they had sailed into was that there was no obvious way out to the sea. Bruno walked to the water edge. There, bobbing up and down against the edge of the ledge was a large glass egg. It had a handle on the side and when Bruno turned it, he was able to lift the top of the egg upwards to reveal a place where 2 people could sit. Below the seats were pedals, similar to those on a bicycle. The boys jumped in and Hamish fastened the lid. Finn had told them that they would need to pedal for the first part of the journey, but once out in the open sea the tide would do the rest. The egg was attached to a thick stainless steel wire cable underneath it that ran all the way from the cave to Marino. The boys used the pedals to move the egg down the wire that would eventually take them right underneath the edge of the cave and out into the open sea. As soon as they dropped below the surface it was easy to see the cable stretching ahead of them out of sight. The boys pedalled carefully and the egg moved slowly along the cable. Once outside of the cave, the tide took over, pushing the egg along quite quickly. The boys laughed at this wonderful new form of transport. They took their feet off the pedals and watched the sea life go by. Initially, it was quite light as they were in fairly shallow water. Hamish looked behind him to see where they had come from and saw the cable stretching back and disappearing into what looked like a cliff that rose up out of the water. He recognised a shoal of sea bass swimming along beside them surging back and forwards with the movement of the waves. Tiny anemones in all colours were clinging to the rocks and they were moving slowly enough to be able to see these properly. Hamish rt about the Dolphin Taxis, and how quickly they travelled. You hardly had time to notice any of the sea life.

The height of the water above them was increasing and the boys noticed that the cable was sloping downwards now quite steeply. Soon they saw the shape of the house ahead. The steel cable ran into a wide hole inside a middle section of the upper floor of the house. Finn had told them to start pedalling as soon as they passed the outside wall of the house, as the cable would start to rise up and they would need to pedal to keep moving.

'This is fun,' Hamish said and smiled. 'It's a bit like going for an underwater bike ride.'

'Yes,' agreed Bruno, who was panting now at the effort of cycling, 'and the road always seems to be uphill!' He laughed.

The egg surfaced through the water and came to a stop against a ledge set in a small room. All the walls were a silver colour, which made it look like something out of a science fiction film. Finn was there to greet them.

'So what do you think about our tide taxi then. Its very environmentally friendly and uses only natural power.'

'Hmm, its not very fast though,' answered Bruno, with a grin on his face.

'No, but good fun and keeps you fit and dry,' added Hamish, wondering who had invented the tide taxi.

'Come on then,' Finn waved his arm,

'Polperro is waiting to talk to you.'

They walked through one of the silver panels which Finn secured tightly behind him, and found themselves in a breathable corridor with water bedrooms to the right and left. One had a double bed in it again attached to the floor with rope and a seaweed style bed cover. One of the walls was covered in starfishes and it looked as if someone had arranged them into a pattern. Finn noticed Bruno staring at them.

'That's my Uncle and Aunt's room. They keep the door closed to stop any unwanted visitors getting in and any visitors they like, getting out. We get a lot of white tipped sharks around here and whilst they're not dangerous, they do like to nibble things. There are two species that are allowed to live in their room. One is the starfish, and every morning my Aunt arranges them into a different shape. She says it's like having a new picture on her wall every day. The second is plankton, which my Aunt catches and adds to her room every day.'

'What is plankton?' Bruno asked,

'It's a tiny fish which glows in the dark. My Aunt hates being in the dark and with a room full of plankton, its quite light in here at night.'

Hamish nudged Bruno grinning. 'Weird,' he muttered, shaking his head, and they moved on down the corridor.

Polperro was waiting for them in the Breathable Room. He looked worried. 'Hello, my friends. He walked up to the boys and put his hands on their shoulders. Thank you for returning to us so swiftly. Do you have good news?'

'Well, we hope so,' answered Bruno slowly. 'We went to the meeting and asked some of the questions that you had written down for us, but on the third question, the man giving the talk got a bit funny and gave us a web site address for more information.'

Polperro guided them to the table. 'And, do you now have the answers we need,' he asked gently.

Hamish answered. 'I think we have. The reason they want to build a new windfarm is that it will be much bigger and easier to make more money whereas it would be difficult and expensive to enlarge the existing one.'

'I see,' said Polperro stroking his beard. Hamish continued. 'They will have to take this wind farm down if the new one goes ahead. He said they might not, but Uncle John says that the new one won't work properly if they don't.'

Bruno took over. 'They have already done

some tests on the seabed and they are putting up something called a wind mast next week which will measure the wind strength and direction in the area.'

Polperro's eyebrows twitched and a smile started to grow across his worried face. 'And do we know where this wind mast is going to be put?'

Bruno took over 'Yes, we do,' he confirmed eagerly. 'We've written down the latitude and longitude which we got from the web site. I hope they're okay, there's no description, just some figures. Here they are.' Bruno took out a piece of paper from his pocket which had the simple figures 50°51'20"N, 05°07'12"W.

'Excellent,' exclaimed Polperro, clapping his hands and standing up. He turned away from them and walked to the other side of the room, nearly standing on a line of crabs that were nibbling on some seaweed in the middle of the floor. 'Well done, both of you. Now we can make a plan.'

Finn, who had said nothing since entering the room, now spoke. 'Shall I get the chart, Polperro?'

'Good idea, Finn. I can show the boys what it all means.'

Finn disappeared through the door, returning minutes later with a large coloured map showing the sea and Oldquay town. Polperro explained that by using the scales on the sides of the chart it was easy to plot the position that the boys had given him. He marked an x at the spot on the chart. It looked to be about 15 miles off the coast just North of Oldquay.

'Ah haa, I see why they have chosen that spot,' exclaimed Polperro, peering at the chart. 'You see these numbers here dotted around the sea area. Well, these show the depth of water in metres, and around the spot we have marked there is a bank of some sort. The water is much shallower there which will make it easier to build on.'

'Thank you boys, you have done your job for us and we are eternally grateful.' Polperro put his hands on each of the boy's shoulders.

'Well, don't you want any more help?' asked Hamish quickly, not wanting to be left out of whatever was now going to happen. 'We could keep in touch and let you know anything we hear and see in the local newspapers.'

'That's very kind of you, but I feel we have asked too much of you already. You have been very brave and you may still get into trouble with your Aunt and Uncle.'

'No, that's not true,' answered Bruno hurriedly. 'We have been very careful and we would like to go on helping. Please.' Bruno had

had the best holiday of his life so far. It would be very boring to go back to the usual beach games that he and Hamish had been playing before they met Finn.

'What will you do now anyway?'

Polperro turned to Finn. 'Could you ask Gupwort and your father to join us please?' Finn nodded and returned with Talon and the same man that had sat opposite the boys when they had had their lunch at Marino.

'Hello again,' Talon said warmly as he came into the room. I gather you have been successful in finding out some information for us. Gupwort just nodded and sat down at the table. Talon looked at Polperro who explained. 'A mast is to be put up here next week which will measure the wind direction and wind speeds in the area. I think we need to think of a way to destroy this mast. I don't mean to harm anybody, but to persuade the windfarm developers that this is perhaps not the right place to build it.'

Finn interrupted. 'But won't they simply put another mast up in its place?'

'Then we would simply destroy it again and again.' If they think there is something unstable about the seabed there or something they cannot understand, they may consider giving up on the idea. I know it seems a bit risky,'

Polperro admitted, 'but we can't just sit here and do nothing while our energy source is being taken away from us, and you never know, it just might work.'

'But how do we destroy something like that,' asked Finn anxiously.

'I think I have an idea.' Gupwort was not as dark as Talon and his eyes were greeny brown. He was also shorter and thinner, and Bruno thought that he really was quite ugly looking. 'They will obviously drill a hole in the seabed and somehow fix the mast into the hole. It will take something or someone with enormous strength to move it, let alone destroy it. But I think we know someone who has that enormous strength.'

'Catapus,' cried Finn excitedly.

'Exactly,' answered Gupwort smiling.

Polperro and Talon nodded and looked at the boys. 'Catapus is a blue whale. She is the largest living thing in our world and she is also a friend of ours. When we want to visit our cousins who live off Kent, she takes us all there. It is too far to swim or to be towed by the dolphins.

'How big is she then?' asked Bruno.

'Well, let's see now,' said Polperro thoughtfully. She would be about the same size as a large aeroplane.

'What, like a large jet you mean?' asked Hamish, his face lighting up with the thought of it.

'Exactly right, young man. Catapus probably has a heart that is bigger than your Aunt's dinghy and that includes the sail, and she probably has arteries that are as wide as our corridors in this house.'

'Wow, that sounds so cool.' Bruno was now jumping on his feet. 'Can we see her?'

'Maybe, and in good time,' answered Polperro. 'Meanwhile we have to work out a plan. Whatever we do will be dangerous and I'm not keen to involve you in it.'

'Oh please Polperro,' Bruno pleaded, nodding at Hamish at the same time. 'We're already involved and we want to help.'

'Very well then. Can you return here in one week's time. Say around teatime. We will need to dismantle the wind mast in the dark, so you will have to find an excuse to get out for the night.'

The boys looked at each other and grinned.

'Now,' said Talon. 'What are you boys doing today? I'm going fishing and could do with some help.'

CHAPTER 12 – Catching a Whopper

The boys pulled on their aquadaptors and swam out of the steel chamber from the Breathable Room. Talon led the way and Finn followed. Once out into the Big Blue, they swam upwards and Bruno saw above them the underside of a large boat. By the time the boys had surfaced, Talon had already pulled himself up onto the deck, which was open at the back of the boat. He lowered a ladder for them. Bruno was amazed at how well muscled and strong Talon was. There wasn't an ounce of flab or fat on him. Talon walked away from them into the little cabin, which sat on the front section of the deck and started the engine before returning to them.

Hamish looked around the deck. 'Where is the net. You don't use rods do you?' he asked.

'Oh, we don't bother too much with the conventional fishing methods.' Hamish noticed Talon winking at Finn as he spoke. 'You'll see what I mean in a minute. You see, we have to feed a lot of hungry mouths but the benefit is that we are at home in the sea and can catch fish easily because we can see them and we are more intelligent than them. For instance, one of the largest fishes in these water is the great white shark.'

'Like Jaws, you mean,' Bruno interrupted.

'Exactly,' Talon answered. There are many of these sharks around these waters but we know they are dangerous to humans and cause a tourist problem on the local beaches if they are seen. So we catch them to eat. Not only do they give us a delicious meal but also we are doing the community a service. Have you ever had Shark soup? Hmm. Its wonderful.' Talon had closed his eyes as if he had just taken a mouthful of something exquisite.

'So, er, are we going to catch a great white shark then,' asked Hamish nervously.

Talon was bending over a large black bucket, which had a mass of fish pieces floating around in a liquid. As Hamish got closer, he saw that the liquid was blood.

'Yuck, that looks disgusting.'

At that moment, Pluto poked his nose out of Hamish's swimming trunks and jumped down onto the ships deck, surprising Talon.

'Now there's some good shark bait.' He laughed at Hamish who quickly picked Pluto off the deck and shoved him back in his pocket.

Talon continued. 'Right, I'm going to move the boat forward and I want you to ladle out the contents behind the boat. Wait until I say so though.' He went back to the wheelhouse and put the engine into gear. The boat moved forward slowly and then started to increase speed. Bruno noticed some fins moving towards the boat and nudged Hamish.

'Dolphins, not sharks,' Hamish laughed. 'They're coming towards us.'

It was Botolph and Osquirt. They knew exactly where the nearest Great White was at any time and were able to direct the boat to the spot. They took their positions just in front of the boat and Talon followed them. After a few minutes, the dolphins broke away and swam to the back of the boat. Talon lifted his right arm and brought it downwards giving the boys the signal to start ladling the fish flesh over the side.

Bruno held the bucket while Hamish and Finn started to ladle the smelly mass over the back of the boat. When they had finished, they stood up and leant against the side deck looking at the trail of bloody mess behind them. Talon had slowed the boat right down. He left the wheelhouse and joined the boys.

'This is the fun part.' He laughed and turned to reach into a wooden locker situated on the left side of the deck. He pulled out something that looked like a sword in a sheath; only it was actually a long knife. Talon attached the sheath around his waist and his left leg so the knife could be quickly drawn from its holder. He then took a long, soft, rope that was coiled up beside the locker, tied a large loop in one end and started to coil it in his left hand.

'It looks like you're going to lasso something,' said Bruno curiously.

'That's right, young man. We won't have long to wait now.' His head remained down as he concentrated on coiling the rope.

Bruno heard a splash behind him. He turned to see the largest mouth he'd ever seen, wide open and just behind the back of the boat. He stepped back quickly as Talon jumped up onto the side deck of the boat and swirled the rope above his head. The Shark turned to look at him and raised his massive body higher out of the water. Talon has been expecting this and hurled the rope over the top of the sharks head, quickly pulling it tight as it fell over the back of his body and caught in front of its large fin. The shark twisted away immediately, and Talon jumped easily onto his scaly back standing either side of his fin and holding onto the rope with his left hand. The shark started to dive, but before the boys lost sight of the two of them, Talon had reached into the sheath and taken out the knife.

'Come on,' shouted Finn. 'You've got to see this.' His eyes gleaming with excitement, he jumped over the back of the boat and disappeared.

Bruno and Hamish looked at each other, neither wanting to admit their fear of being in the water with this massive fish. Their minds were quickly made up as Pluto suddenly dropped from Hamish's pocket, ran quickly to the back edge of the boat and disappeared over the side.

'Pluto, come back,' cried Hamish, who dived straight in after him. Bruno was left alone on the boat in two minds whether to join the others. The shark had looked terrifying, but on the other hand, Talon and Finn had done this hundreds of times before. He stepped to the edge of the deck and dived in.

Hamish and Finn were just below him keeping very still. Some way away, Bruno could see the Shark moving quickly around in circles. Talon was riding him as if he was standing on the back of a stallion. The shark would twist and turn to try and get Talon off, but it was no use. After a few minutes Bruno noticed that the shark had slowed down. Talon was sitting now, astride his back in front of his fin, and by wrapping his legs around the body of the shark, he was able to keep his balance. Bruno noticed the bright gleam of the knife handle sticking out of the Shark's head. There was no blood, and yet the shark was definitely slowing down.

Finn swam over to join Talon. The shark had

stopped moving and between the two of them, they gently let the shark fall onto the seabed. Finn removed the rope noose from around the body and they both swam up to the surface. Pluto was now swimming around the dead shark as if he was interested in tasting him, so Hamish swam down and grabbed him before Talon noticed.

Bruno and Hamish surfaced before the others and climbed back onto the boat.

'I wish I could do that.' Bruno turned to Hamish. 'I can't even catch a fish with a rod!'

'You can do that,' Hamish replied. 'After all, Talon knew where the shark was. If you'd known exactly where a sea bass was, poured a cup of worms on top of him and been able to breathe as well as he could underwater, I expect you could have done just as good a job.' He laughed and nudged his friend affectionately.

Bruno nodded and smiled. 'Yeah, but it was quite cool, wasn't it.?' His voice full of admiration.

By now, Talon and Finn had pulled themselves up onto the deck and were pulling a large canvas sheet out of the locker. It had straps coming from all sides and there were long pieces of seaweed, which had been rolled into rope strands and attached down the length of the sheet every couple of inches.

'Do you want to give us a hand? The Mistress of the Kitchen and her team will be along in the minute to take our dinner home, but they can always do with some extra help.'

The boys nodded and they all dived back into the water. The shark lay very still but Hamish thought he looked alive. Certainly his eye was open and was looking at him.

Talon had brought down with him a small balloon attached to a long line. He passed the line under the shark's body and pulled it out on the other side. Then tied it back onto the balloon. He pulled a small canister from his pocket and put the nozzle onto a fitting on the end of the balloon and pressed a switch on the canister. The balloon inflated and slowly, the shark was raised off the seabed. Only a few feet, but enough for them to pass the big canvas sheet under the shark's body and wrap it around him. They brought the sides together and clipped them together using the straps. Just as they had finished doing this, Bruno noticed some movement to his left. Swimming towards them was a team of Gillanders led by Botolph and Osquirt. Next, Bruno noticed a very large and important looking woman who was wearing an apron over her wet suit. She had long grey hair and was probably as old as his grandmother. Behind her were Coral and

Nemone and behind them a number of men and women. The older woman who Bruno presumed to be the Mistress of the Kitchen motioned for the others to stop while she swam over the shark and then around it. She then gestured to the others who took up their places around the great fish, each one taking one of the seaweed lines hanging from the sheet now wrapped around the Shark. Botolph and Osquirt took the lines at the front.

Finn gesticulated to Hamish and Bruno to take one of the spare lines at the back, and the procession moved off. They moved quite quickly as the weight of the shark was taken by the air filled balloon that was holding it above the seabed. Bruno felt very important and swam quickly so that he felt he was doing his fair share of the pulling.

Very soon the procession came into sight of the House. Osquirt and Botolph directed them around the back and into what looked like a large garage. Finn grabbed a small piece of coral as they went in and popped the balloon, so that the Shark settled on the floor of the room. The garage door was lowered. It was noisy and Bruno was pleased to be following the others through a water passage into a steel chamber similar to the one used to get into the breathable room. He held onto the rail at the side, and once everyone was ready, Finn flicked the switch and the water started to disappear out of the bottom. The Mistress of the Kitchen was the first to speak.

'Thank you for your help boys. Will you be staying for supper?'

Bruno was taken aback by her deep voice and he was still unused to her large size. He shook his head. 'Er no, we'll have to be getting back unfortunately,' he answered looking at Hamish.

'Oh, what a shame. You'll have to have a fishy bag then.' She climbed out of the chamber followed by the rest of the team and Bruno and Hamish followed them. The chamber was situated in the corner of the kitchen. When Bruno turned round, having climbed over the wall of the chamber, he couldn't believe his eyes. The whole kitchen was moving. There were large containers all around the room, filled with live fish of all shapes and sizes. Lobsters and crabs were racing around the floor and occasionally one of the kitchen team would bend down and pick one of these up, plunging it into a pot of boiling water or simply piercing its head with a spike. Bruno watched as the Mistress of the Kitchen opened one of the cupboards set back on the wall. Cockles and snails poured out on top of her and fell onto the floor. Within seconds they were out of their shells and moving away from her feet looking for their escape.

As he tried to cross the room he nearly trod on a large eel that slithered its way across the floor.

'Moray Eel,' said Hamish taking a step back, 'Watch out.'

'Scaley!' The Mistress of the Kitchen shouted loudly looking around her. Her voice booming across the room. Everyone stopped and stood still. A small old man moved towards her. He looked more of a fish than a man, with fish scales all over his arms. He had a pointed nose and ears that sloped backwards. He was bald except for one line of hair on the centre of his head.

'Yes, ma lady,' he answered quietly.

'Why are the live shellfish in the cupboards, how many times do I have to tell you. Cupboards for the dead and drawers for the live,' she said crossly.

'Yes, ma lady. I knew it to be one or the other. I must have got it wrong again.' Scaley shrugged.

Finn winked at the boys. 'Come on, let's get out of here.'

CHAPTER 13 – The excitement grows

Before leaving Marino, the Mistress of the Kitchen had sent up a large bag for the boys to take away. It was a piece of the shark and smelt delicious. Bruno put the bag on the kitchen table the moment they arrived home.

'What have we here? You didn't catch anything, did you Bruno?' asked Auntie Moo in surprise.

'No, we were fishing in the harbour though and a fishing boat came in. They had caught a Great White Shark and gave us some,' answered Bruno who had already prepared his story.

Auntie Moo laughed. 'That's a good one. Was it Jaws?'

'Honestly, Auntie Moo, there are Great Whites out there,' said Hamish firmly.

'Well, let's have a look shall we. I know most of the fresh fish round here.' She opened the bag and put the large chunk of fish onto a plate.

'Well, I must admit, it looks most unusual, and they've cooked it already. I wonder why they did that. Anyway it will be very nice for our supper.'

Suddenly, Pluto jumped up onto the table, almost at the same time as Bosun arrived. The two looked at each other and the fish plate between them. Auntie Moo, who was standing a few feet away, stepped forward and reached down to grab the plate. Too late, Bosun had lunged at it. Grabbed the shark piece and jumped off the table. He disappeared out of the kitchen with Pluto in pursuit.

Auntie Moo charged after them. 'Bosun, bring that fish back now. That's not for you.' She rounded the corner of the lounge to see Pluto lying in front of her desk, his long green tail thumping the floor. Bosun was under the desk with the fish in his mouth, growling and hissing through his teeth, and bringing his front leg up to protect himself when Pluto tried to get close.

'Bosun, drop it.' Auntie Moo had no hesitation in reaching out under the desk and grabbing Bosun by the scruff of his neck. Bruno and Hamish had following her into the lounge and watched as Bosun screamed like a wild tiger and lashed out with his claws. But he eventually dropped the fish. Auntie Moo picked it up and released Bosun who hissed at her and slunk off into the hall.

Hamish picked Pluto up and put him quickly back in his pocket. 'Well, Bosun and Pluto think the fish smells nice anyway,' he laughed.

Hamish and Bruno tried to make themselves

busy for the next week. They were so excited about the thought of seeing Catapus the whale that they almost forgot to think of an excuse to be away for the evening. They were out on the rocks fishing when they realised they only had 2 days left to come up with an excuse.

'Auntie Moo is not going to let us stay out till midnight,' said Bruno miserably once they had sat down and thought about it. 'And anyway, I can't think of anything that we should be doing till that time.'

'What about asking if we could spend the night in a tent on the cliffs that night. It would be reasonable to set off in the afternoon to find a good spot,' suggested Hamish.

Bruno shook his head. 'They'll never let us do that. There are all those stories of kids disappearing in the newspapers and I know that Auntie Moo will feel too responsible.'

'How about we go and stay with someone then,' Hamish asked. He too was realising that this wasn't going to be easy.

'We don't know anyone down here, and they aren't likely to let us stay with someone we've just met anyway.'

'We've only got 2 more days to think about it or else we'll have to tell them we can't come.' Bruno faced Hamish with a serious look on his face.

'Hello,' said a loud voice from the sea. It was Finn. He climbed out onto the rocks.

'I'm glad you're here,' said Finn. 'We are changing arrangements for Thursday. We thought it would be better to meet out there just as it gets light so that we can see what we're doing. That'll be around 3.00ish in the morning. We were wondering if you might be able to come by boat, as it might be helpful to have you on the water if something goes wrong. What do you think?'

Hamish grinned. 'That sounds like a much better idea. If we leave the house in the middle of the night, we won't have to tell my Aunt and Uncle anything. We can come down here, launch Wishful and meet you out there.'

'Hang on a minute.' Bruno raised one of his hands. 'You know we can't get Wishful into the water without help if the tide is out. Finn, do you know what time high tide is on Thursday?'

'Yes, its at midnight, so you'll have no trouble getting her into the water. '

'Sounds good to me,' said Hamish smiling. It really was going to happen. They would see the whale. 'So we need to leave here around 1.30 ish.'

'Hmm, I've just thought of something,' Finn frowned. 'You won't know where to sail to and it will be difficult in the dark. I'll send Botolph to help you. He can guide you there if there's wind, or tow you if there isn't.'

Bruno could hardly contain his excitement, 'But will we see the whale if we're not in the water,' he asked eagerly.

'I'll bring some aquadaptors for you anyway. We might need everyone underwater. Do you have an anchor for your boat?' asked Finn.

Bruno nodded. 'I've seen one in the forward locker, but I've never used it.'

'Good. That's settled,' said Finn sounding very grown up. 'We'll meet you there around 2.30 ish. If you have any problems, Botolph will simply return without you, and I'll know that you couldn't make it.'

'We'll be there,' shouted the boys together. Bruno added. 'The only reason that we won't come is if the weather is bad. Will you go ahead with your plan in bad weather?'

'That depends. Underwater is usually quite peaceful whatever the wind is doing. The forecast is fine anyway so hopefully, see you then.' Finn waved as he dived into the water and disappeared.

Auntie Moo had frozen the shark and brought it out for the family's supper.

'You don't seem very hungry, either of you.'

111

Auntie Moo cleared away the plates with half the fish still left on them. 'Have you been buying sweets or something,' she asked laughing.

'Eh, no. I'm just not very hungry at the moment. Would it be possible to take a sandwich to my room in case I get hungry later?' Bruno asked.

Auntie Moo looked at him and frowned.' Well, I suppose there's no harm in that.' She wondered whether the boys were planning a midnight feast and didn't want to say anything. 'I'll make you some peanut butter and jam then. Presumably Hamish would like some too?'

'Yes please. Its funny, but I'm not hungry at the moment either,' he said nervously. They both knew they were too excited to eat, and her suggestion of a sandwich which they could take on the boat was very lucky. 'And could we have something to drink as well?'

Auntie Moo smiled as she buttered the bread. 'Yes, Yes, and some chocolate biscuits I suppose. I don't know why you didn't like the fish. I thought it was delicious. I'm still not sure what kind of fish it is though.'

Bruno looked at Hamish and grinned. He put his thumb up and climbed down from the table.

'Does that mean you're going to have a party in your room tonight Bruno?' Paisley asked. She was just finishing her spaghetti having refused to join the family in the Shark meal. She had carefully hidden the ham pieces that Auntie Moo had insisted on adding to the cheese sauce under her spoon.

'No, why do you ask?' answered Bruno guiltily.

'I think you are, and I want to come too,' Paisley voice turned into a whine.

Auntie Moo noticed the pile of ham. 'Paisley, couldn't you eat some of that ham. I only gave you a tiny amount. '

'I don't like ham.' Paisley's bottom lip started to tremble.

'Okay, okay, leave it then. It's just that you've hardly eaten anything!' Auntie Moo sighed.

'More than the boys.' Paisley said sharply.

Hamish snorted, lifting his eyes to the ceiling. His cousin could be impossible at times.

'Right, its bath night for all of you. So get a move on.' Auntie Moo herded the three towards the door. 'Uncle John's got a day off tomorrow so I thought we'd all do something together. This is the last opportunity before you go back next week. It would be nice if you all had an early night and are fresh for tomorrow.' Bruno and Hamish smiled at each other as they climbed the stairs.

CHAPTER 14 – So many heroes

Hamish had set his alarm for midnight and put it under his duvet so it wouldn't wake anyone else. He was in a deep sleep, swimming with Osquirt and Botolph. He was holding onto both of them. One on each side and they were swimming together very fast so that it was difficult to hang on. He could see a large shape in front but couldn't work out what it was. Just as it came into view, the alarm went off. He sat up in bed wondering where he was and then realised, fumbling for the clock under his duvet.

'Are you awake Bruno?' he whispered.

'Yes, I've been awake most of the night. I couldn't sleep.'

'Come on then, let's go,' replied Hamish pulling on his clothes, '… and don't forget the picnic.'

They turned the handle on their bedroom door and pulled it open to peer outside onto the landing. Their bedroom was at the front of the house very close to the staircase and Auntie Moo and Uncle John slept at the back of the house. They tiptoed out and down the stairs. As they got half way down, they heard a door open and saw Paisley appear at the top of the stairs.

'Where are you going?' she whispered.

'Ssh,' answered Bruno raising two of his

fingers to his mouth. He waved her down the stairs into the kitchen and shut the door behind her. This was going to be difficult. She would want to come with them.

'Paisley, you shouldn't be up, it's very late,' Bruno scolded.

'Where are you going?' she repeated, emphasizing the word "going".

'Just out and you can't come, you're too young.'

Bruno saw tears well in Paisley's eyes.

'Look, we're going out on a sort of adventure and it's going to be …. difficult, well dangerous maybe, and you'll be frightened.'

'Won't.' said Paisley stubbornly, 'And anyway, if you don't let me come, I'm going to wake Auntie Moo.'

'Oh no,' groaned Hamish. 'Let her come. We need to go now and we're just wasting time. She can sit in the bottom of the boat and go to sleep. Paisley, get a jumper and a jacket, and a blanket if you can find one. But be quick and be quiet.'

Paisley cheered up and crept out of the kitchen door.

'This is not a good idea,' said Bruno screwing up his face.

'No, but there's no choice,' shrugged Hamish. 'She will tell Auntie Moo. It's the only way.'

There was no wind, and no clouds. The moon was bright and gave them some light, which helped whilst they walked down the sandy path to the beach. Hamish and Bruno quickly peeled off Wishful's cover and made her ready for the sea. Paisley put her lifejacket on and stood looking out over the water.

'Will we see the dolphins?' she asked.

'Yes, Botolph is coming to meet us,' answered Hamish. 'He will tow us out to sea if there's not enough wind.'

Paisley beamed. She loved the dolphins and knew she would be safe with them.

They pushed Wishful down the beach and into the water. Bruno lifted Paisley over the side and held the boat while Hamish walked the trailer back up the beach. They pushed the boat out and jumped in over the stern. Hamish scrambled forward to pull in the jib in case there was any wind to push them along.

'I think we should use the paddle,' Bruno whispered, 'there's hardly any wind, and no-one will hear us tonight.'

Hamish took the paddle, which was lying in the bottom of the boat and started paddling the boat out to sea. At that moment, they heard the familiar dolphin chatter. Botolph appeared just in front of them, his head out of the water.

'Hello Botolph, I think we're going to need your help. Hamish, hang the painter over the bow of the boat, can you?'

Botolph put his nose through the loop of the rope, and they were off. Bruno sat in silence, steering the boat while Hamish explained to Paisley about the wind farm and how they were going to try and take the mast down with the whale's help.

Bruno interrupted. 'When we get there Paisley, you must stay in the boat and behave. It's going to be dangerous and you have to be very grown up.' Paisley nodded. She knew Bruno was furious with her anyway and she didn't want to upset him any more.

It took about one hour to get out to the mast. Hamish unwrapped the picnic which they shared between the three of them, and Bruno started to relax. He knew they wouldn't see anything until they got out to the mast, as the Gillanders would all be underwater making preparations. Osquirt would be on the lookout for their arrival and would alert Finn. Bruno had been thinking about the plan over the last couple of days and he wondered how they would be able to get the mast down.

The glow of the sun was just starting to show

over the horizon as they arrived at the mast. Finn was in the water waving and beckoned them over to him. He pulled himself over the side and into the boat. He was wearing a thick rubber suit and had flippers on. He pulled a large bag behind him.

'Don't look so surprised, even we get cold in the middle of the night down there, and the flippers help to give us speed and strength. Anyway, how did it all go?' He noticed Paisley sitting quietly by the mast. 'Oh Paisley, I didn't know you were coming.'

'She insisted,' Hamish answered for her. 'There was nothing we could do about it.'

'Ah, I see, well I'll get Botolph to go and pick up an extra suit and aquadaptors for her. Here is your stuff. There's a warm wet suit for each of you and a pair of aquadaptors each. If you give me your anchor, I'll take it down and wedge it behind a rock.'

Hamish climbed forward past Paisley and put his hand under the small deck just in front of the mast. He felt a cold metal rod. 'I've got it.' He pulled out a small silver coloured anchor with a long rope attached to one end.

'Tie the end of the rope onto that ring right on the front of the boat.' Finn instructed. 'And then pass me the anchor.' He dived into the water and took the anchor from Hamish. Bruno had already changed into his wetsuit and boots and was tidying up the sails. Botolph appeared with another wetsuit and aquadaptors for Paisley. Hamish pulled on his wetsuit whilst Bruno explained that Paisley would be more useful keeping watch in the boat. She would be warmer and safer as well.

'I can swim just as well as Hamish,' she argued, 'and I don't want to be alone out here,' she added defiantly.

Bruno looked at Hamish who shrugged. 'Well, you know the story of Moby Dick. Maybe Catapus will breathe in too hard and Paisley will end the evening as her dinner.' Hamish winked at Bruno.

'I saw that wink Hamish. I don't know who Moby Dick is, but I'm sure I can look after myself just as well as you can.' Paisley was pulling on her wetsuit and boots whilst speaking. Before the boys could say any more she jumped into the water and disappeared. Bruno and Hamish followed.

They swam down to the seabed where they could see a group of Gillanders swimming around. A large rope had been attached to the mast just above the place where it came out of the rock. The other end disappeared out of sight. Finn met them and beckoned for them to follow him. He followed the line of the rope and Bruno saw an enormous grey wall looming out of the darkness ahead of him. Only this wall was moving, slowly, away from the rope. Bruno stopped in amazement and held his hand out for Paisley. Catapus was a gigantic creature, with an eye as big as a large tractor wheel, gazing out at them. She had the rope looped around the front part of her body and she was slowly edging forward tightening the rope. Finn moved back from the whale and motioned for the boys and Paisley to follow. The other Gillanders arrived to join them. Bruno noticed Gupwort amongst the group and waved to him. He grinned, waved back and swam up to the whale's eye. He seemed to be talking to Catapus and finally put his thumb and forefinger together make an 'o'shape, as if he was saying okay to the whale. Gupwort then swam back to the group.

Catapus moved her enormous tail downwards to move herself forward. The rope became tight. She carried on moving her tail and started using her side fins as well. Nothing happened. She started to twist her body now using the power of her massive weight to propel herself. Still the mast did not budge.

Gupwort swam back to Catapus and positioned himself close to the whale's eye. He used his hands gesticulating as if he were using a sign language and Catapus lay quietly until he had finished. Gupwort returned to the group. The whale moved backwards towards the mast until the rope lay along the seabed now loose. Suddenly, Catapus started moving her tail. She propelled her great body forward at a frightening speed. The rope started to tighten. As the rope became taught there was a loud graunching noise and then quiet. Catapus disappeared out of sight. The rope had broken.

Gupwort shrugged his shoulders, looked around at all the faces now facing towards him anxiously and pointed to the surface.

The whole group surfaced, but only Finn, the boys, Paisley and Gupwort got into the dinghy.

'What now?' asked Finn looking at Gupwort.

'I'm not sure. The angle is all wrong,' answered Gupwort. 'We are pulling against the rock that is holding the mast in place. I think we need to attach a rope higher up the mast so that when it is pulled over the mast will snap where it goes into the rock. But how do we get up there?'

Bruno remembered looking at the Oldquay windfarm website.

'Isn't there a platform that goes all around the mast at approximately 10 metres high? I'm not sure how high that is but if we could get onto it we could easily tie a rope there.'

'Yes,' cried Finn, 'And the spout from a blue whale can reach 10 metres, so if Catapus lies on the water and blows, her spout could reach the platform. All we need is someone very light to be lifted up by it,' he added excitedly. They all looked at each other and slowly one by one turned to look at Paisley.

'What?' she said pretending she hadn't been listening. 'Why are you all looking at me?'

'Because you're as light as a feather!' answered Bruno.

'So, what is a spout anyway?' Paisley asked slowly.

'It's the water jet that comes out of the hole on Catapus's head,' said Finn laughing. 'You could sit on her head and she'll blow you up onto the platform.'

'What happens if I fall off?' said Paisley nervously.

'Catapus is very gentle and careful. She won't let that happen,' answered Finn.

Bruno interrupted 'Yes, and you did want to do something out here. This is a real way you can help. If the spout isn't high enough, she can just lower you down onto her head again.'

There was a niggling in the back of Bruno's head. He knew he shouldn't be allowing her to do this, but Paisley was a natural gymnast. She was top of her gym class and had had extra tuition since she was 4 years old. She was the ideal person to go up there.

Paisley nodded and a large beam appeared on her face. She wanted to be involved and this was obviously a very important part of the job.

Finn dived overboard to get Catapus and to explain the plan to the other Gillanders.

Gupwort moved closer to Paisley. 'Right then Paisley. We will ask Catapus to blow as hard as she can to get you as high as possible up the mast. If you can grab hold of the railings around the platform you might be able to pull yourself onto the platform, but don't try to be too brave. Are you quite strong?'

'Oh yes, I'm top of my Gym Class,' she said proudly. 'I can easily swing onto the platform if I can grip the rail.'

'Good, and can you climb down a rope?' asked Gupwort.

Paisley nodded. Bruno looked up at Gupwort. 'She'll be fine, she's very fit and we've been climbing ropes since we were able to walk.'

'Excellent. We will tie a rope around you so that when you get onto the platform you simply take it through the railing, around the mast and drop it back to us. When we have it, we will hold both ends and you can climb down one. Is that Okay?'

Paisley nodded and looked over towards the mast platform. It was still dark but there was a glow in the sky behind her and she could make out the shadow of the mast. The platform looked quite high but she could easily come down a rope from there.

Finn arrived back and hauled himself into the boat. Catapus will be coming alongside in a minute. We think it's best if Paisley lies on her tummy so she can reach out for the railings easily. Also it will be the best way to balance on the water spout.'

Paisley stood up and moved across the boat to where Finn was standing. She looked over the side and saw a dark shape under the water. It moved and surfaced right beside the boat. Catapus was about nine times the size of Wishful and Paisley could see her great eye looking up at her. She shivered. Finn tied a rope around her waist and pointed out the blowhole just behind Catapus's eye. The whale's skin was very odd as Paisley crawled across her scaly back to the blowhole. It was a bit like wet leather but more slippery. She lay across the blowhole, as Finn had explained, with her arms and legs splayed out wide. She felt her whole body tighten with excitement a bit like she felt when visiting the funfair.

Catapus moved away from the boat towards the mast. Suddenly Paisley heard a noise, similar to the one she had heard out at sea, during the first week they had arrived in Cornwall, when the sea was covered in fog. At the same time she felt a spurt of water under her chest and tummy and realised she was moving off the whale's back and up into the air. Slowly she went higher and higher. Catapus seemed to be in complete control, and Paisley became mesmerised by the whole experience. She forgot to be frightened and it was only when she saw the railings of the platform close to her left hand that she remembered what she had to do. She grabbed hold of the railings and quickly swung her body around on the spout so that she could get a hold with her other hand. Catapus was still supporting her and Paisley found that with the spout underneath her she could easily haul herself over the top of the railings. She landed on her feet on the platform and stood up. There was a shout from the boat. Bruno was waving and shouted. 'Well done little sis. That was fantastic.' She waved back. Finn had told her to be as quiet as she could be, as sound could carry from that height back to the shore. She untied the rope from round her waist and put it through one of the railing struts.

Then she turned and walked around the platform, which took her behind the mast and back again until she arrived at the same place she had landed where the rope came through the railing. She then hung the end out over the sea and pulled more and more rope up from one side so that she could let more and more down into the sea.

By this time, the boys were in the water below and Hamish grabbed the rope as it came down. Gupwort took the rope going up and they signalled to Paisley that it was safe for her to climb down. This was not going to be as easy as she had thought. She needed to climb over the railings before she could get hold of the rope, which was below her feet at this point. She lifted one leg over, changed her handgrip and then lifted her other leg over. Below Bruno looked up anxiously.

'Wrap your feet round the rope now,' he called up as loudly as he dared.

Paisley lowered herself onto the rope still with both hands holding onto the rail. She felt for the rope with her right foot and knew that Bruno would let it loose below so she could wrap the rope around her leg first. They both climbed ropes together so many times and she trusted him totally. Bruno loosened it as she expected and Paisley was able to get a good hold with her right foot and used her left foot to act as a brake on the rope. Once in this position, she used the railing struts to lower herself slowly down the rope until she could grab the rope with both hands. The rest was simple and she quickly climbed down to Bruno in the water who gave her a big hug.

'You are such a brave and clever girl. I'm really pleased with you. '

Paisley beamed at her brother. This sort of praise was very unusual. Bruno was usually telling her what a spoilt, and useless sister she was.

Gupwort had disappeared and Bruno, Hamish and Paisley ducked down into the water to see what was happening. They could see Catapus below them and Gupwort was looping the rope over her head. He looked up and motioned them to move away from the mast. They swam over to where the rest of the Gillanders had collected in a group all swimming around slowly facing Catapus. Gupwort swum over to join them and signalled to Catapus. The whole group then swam up to the surface. The rope, which was now attached to the platform, was being pulled taught by Catapus who was slowly moving away from the mast.

'Look,' cried Bruno unable to hide his

excitement, 'It's bending!' The bottom of the mast had started to bend towards Catapus who was still moving slowly away from it. Suddenly there was a loud cracking noise and it looked as if the whole mast came away from its foundations. It simply fell into the water.

'Let's go underwater,' said Finn excitedly and dived out of sight. The others followed. The mast had broken at the place where it disappeared into the rock. Just as Gupwort had said it would. Finn looked at Bruno and raised a thumb, which Bruno took to mean something like 'We've done it.'

Catapus's tail could be seen in the distance. A large T shaped shadow the size of a hotel. Quite frightening, Bruno thought, and then put it out of his mind. He knew Catapus was friendly but she was so enormous, it was difficult to feel friendly back. Finn beckoned to him and swam over towards the tail in the distance. Bruno followed with Paisley swimming close to his feet and Bruno taking up the back position. When they arrived at Catapus's tail, Bruno could make out the long back of the whale stretching away from him and saw that the rope was still wrapped around her body behind her head. He could see there was a problem. In pulling on the loop so hard, the rope had pulled back against her flesh and tightened as she pulled. It was now very definitely stuck and Catapus was becoming agitated. Gupwort was swimming around her trying hopelessly to pull on the rope. He signalled for the group to surface.

'We need to get help quickly,' Gupwort explained. 'The rope is strangling her and she hasn't got enough freedom to swim to the surface. Do you have a knife in your boat?

Bruno shook his head 'I've got a Swiss Army Knife in my pack in Wishful, but the blade would take ages to cut through that rope. It's too thick.'

Below them, they heard a moaning sound. At first, it was just a little moan and then it got louder, almost a roar. Gupwort disappeared underwater to try and soothe her.

He returned quickly. 'We've got to do something or else she will die.' he shouted to Finn above the moaning.

Finn frowned. 'Ah, maybe the lobster family that live with Polperro can help. I'll get Osquirt to fetch them.'

He disappeared below the water leaving the rest of them looking at each other in silence. Bruno shrugged. 'What can they do?'

'Well, they do have sharp pincers, but like your knife, a lobster will take ages to get through that rope. Let's go down and see what's happening.' Gupwort suggested.

Bruno could see that Catapus was now in a lot of pain. Her eyes kept closing and she kept writhing around. There was no sign of Finn and he wondered if they would be in time to save her. He was also conscious of the time. It was a quarter past 4 and he felt they ought to be getting back to the beach. Whilst his Aunt and Uncle weren't early risers, his Uncle often woke earlier in the summer as their bedroom faced East and the sun would pour through the curtains even though Auntie Moo had sewn a thick lining material onto the back of them. He caught Hamish's attention and pointed at his watch. Hamish shrugged and pointed at Catapus. Bruno knew he wanted to stay and help. Before he could make a decision, he noticed Osquirt racing towards Catapus with a seaweed bag in his mouth. Osquirt laid the bag on Catapus's back and within seconds, about fifty of the largest lobsters Bruno had ever seen crawled out and were gnawing at the rope. They were all very close together and you could see the rope weaken, even though it was not cut all the way through, the lobsters attack was allowing the rope to stretch and Catapus started to relax. After a minute, the largest lobster had cut through the rope completely. They all lay on the whales back exhausted. Catapus couldn't wait though; she swished her tail and suddenly her whole body accelerated forward and out of the water as if in one movement. The lobsters fell onto the seabed in a heap, most of them on their backs. Their thin legs flailing above them trying to manoeuvre themselves back onto their right sides again. Bruno noticed Paisley was trying not to laugh, and had to smile himself. The seabed was a mass of movement and he swam down closer to get a better look. Hundreds of lobsters and crabs were moving in from every direction. They were all making for the lobsters that had helped Catapus. As soon as the first crabs got there, those that were on their backs were gently helped to turn over. Bruno watched in astonishment as the mass of shellfish raised the exhausted lobsters above their heads and formed a procession along the seabed as if to honour these special heroes. Other fish were also arriving on the scene. Large Cod, Sea bass, and small Tuna joined in giving the procession protection from above and swimming slowly as the whole group made their way eastwards presumably Bruno thought towards Marino. Bruno saw a Moray Eel slither up alongside the procession and some of the smaller crabs hitched a ride on his back. Bruno, Paisley and Hamish had stopped swimming and floated motionless above the spectacle. Paisley couldn't believe her eyes, and couldn't wait to get back to tell Auntie Moo. Her expression of delight turned to dismay once she remembered that she wouldn't be able to tell anyone about this. Would she be able to keep all this a secret, she wondered.

Bruno pointed to his watch again, and Hamish nodded. Reluctantly, they swam to the surface. Paisley holding onto her older brother's leg so that she could continue to watch the procession on the way up.

Finn was waiting on the surface.

'Wasn't that amazing?' cried Bruno. 'Those lobsters were real heroes.'

Finn nodded and smiled. 'Yes, but the real award for the day goes to Paisley and you two.' He looked at Bruno and Hamish. Without your help over the last three weeks and Paisley's tonight, none of this would have been possible. It isn't over yet anyway, they may decide to put up another mast.'

'What will happen then?' asked Paisley seriously.

'We'll just have to pull it down again,' answered Finn smiling. 'Come on, you are going to be late home. Botolph is waiting to take you. Can you let us know what the papers say? '

'Yeah, but when will we meet again?' Bruno asked.

'I'll come to the rocks the day after tomorrow. You can go fishing there. Where we first met.'

CHAPTER 15 – A Change of Plan

They climbed back into Wishful. The sun was now well up above the horizon and Bruno thought that they might be seen coming back into the beach. He suggested to Hamish that they put the sails up despite the fact that Botolph would be towing them in as it might be odd seeing a boat moving quickly through the water without sails or engine. Hamish quickly raised the mainsail and unfurled the little jib. Paisley, who had been promoted since her help on the mast, was allowed to go forward onto Wishful's foredeck and hang the loop of rope over the front for Botolph to put his nose through.

'It might be better if you hide Paisley. At least that way no-one will be able to tell that it was us in the boat if we are seen.'

'Oooh,' said Paisley in a whiney voice. Why can't Hamish hide, I want to watch Botolph.' Bruno raised his eyes. 'Let's just leave it then, if we're caught, we just went for an early morning sail.' He looked at Hamish. They both knew that no one would believe this story anyway and they would be in big trouble if they were caught.

They were making good headway across the water but were still a long way away when Hamish pointed to the beach. 'Oh no!' They could just make out a dark shape on the road above the beach and a blue flashing light.

Hamish and Paisley looked at Bruno. He looked from one to the other. His usual frown deepening across his forehead. 'Drop the sails. Quick.' Hamish obeyed immediately although he couldn't understand how that would help. 'Paisley, take the helm.'

'I don't know how to,' whispered Paisley. Her braveness of the last couple of hours seemed to have left her and she was now thinking of the trouble they were in.

'Just hold this stick, keep it pointing to the front of the boat.' Bruno was now shouting. He leapt forward, and lifted Paisley behind him. He crawled onto the foredeck and called to Botolph. The dolphin was swimming ahead of them under about 2 ft of water, but heard Bruno immediately. He surfaced and made his usual chattering noise as if talking to them. 'Botolph, can you take us to the cave?' Bruno asked the dolphin gravely. Botolph's head moved up and down as if nodding. 'We'll need to go quickly and we are going to lie down in the boat so no one will be able to see us on the beach. Do you understand? There is trouble on the beach.' Botolph nodded again and slipped beneath the surface.

Bruno jumped back into the boat and took

over from Paisley. 'Both of you lie down in the bottom of the boat like this.' He slid down the side of the bench seat and lay against the wooden slats across the bottom of the boat. His arm sticking up holding onto the tiller.

'What's the plan?' whispered Hamish, from his lying position just behind the mast.

'Don't really know. That police car could be there for any reason. It might be nothing to do with us. But whatever happens we will be seen if we try to come into the beach now and we'll be in real trouble. If we could somehow get back to the house and into our rooms without being seen, no one will know we've been out. We can leave Wishful in the cave for now and bring her round later. That is provided that no-one realises she has disappeared.'

Hamish frowned. 'Sounds like wishful thinking to me!'

'But Wishful's a boat. She doesn't think,' whispered Paisley from her position on the floor.

'Hmm. Well it gives us time to think. I don't know the answer at the moment. Perhaps Finn could help,' answered Bruno. 'Hamish, can you find the binoculars, which are usually kept in a yellow waterproof container in the locker just by your head.'

Bruno aimed the binoculars at the beach. He

could see the police car clearly with its flashing blue light. There were four people standing on the beach looking out to sea and Bruno knew they would easily be seen from that distance. Botolph was towing them fast now and soon they would be round the point and out of sight. He lay back down in the boat.

'I suppose they'll call out a police boat. I hope we get to the cave before that arrives,' he stated gravely.

Paisley was looking frightened and lay quietly in her corner beside Hamish. Finally they were out of sight of the beach. Bruno sat up to see if he could see the opening of the cave. He had forgotten that they had always had help finding it. Then he realised that Botolph would know the way. He was thinking about what he was going to say to his Uncle and Aunt and wondered whether he could tell them the truth. Auntie Moo would probably believe him but Uncle John would just get cross. No, that wasn't going to be a good idea. Better to pretend they had all gone off for an early morning swim.

Botolph guided the little boat carefully into the cave and shook off the rope. He chattered to them as if to say goodbye and then swam out to the open sea. Hamish leapt ashore and tied Wishful to the cave ledge as before.

'Where are we?' asked Paisley, her eyes open wide in amazement.

'In a secret cave that Finn uses when he wants to come ashore. Come on, we've got to hurry,' answered Hamish.

They leapt onto the ledge and climbed up in the tunnel. Bruno almost dragging Paisley behind him. There seemed to be more light in the tunnel than when they had used it before and they were able to run all the way to the rock door at the end. Hamish jumped on the rock and the door slid open. Paisley stopped to put her arm across her face to shade her eyes from the bright light outside but Bruno pulled her through.

'Come on Paisley,' he said roughly. 'Hurry up.'

The three of them raced down the cliff path stumbling and puffing. When they got to the house, they looked up at Auntie Moo and Uncle John's bedroom.

'Funny,' whispered Bruno. 'The curtains are still drawn. Tread quietly.'

They tiptoed to the back door and let themselves in using the key, which Bruno knew was always kept in the flat cap hanging on a hook in the shed. He replaced the key after opening the door. The kitchen was empty and there was no sign of anyone having got up.

Bruno looked at the clock. Twenty past six. He waved to the others to follow him and they tiptoed up the stairs. No one noticed Pluto who had jumped out of Hamish's pocket and started walking down the hall corridor.

Bruno pointed to Paisley's door as they reached the top of the stairs and put both his hands to one side of his face to suggest she get into bed. Once he had seen her safely close her door, the boys went into their own room and closed the door.

CHAPTER 16 – A law abiding place to sleep

He was in the water helping to saw through the rope around Catapus's body when his heart missed a beat. A shark had appeared and was circling them. Finn had also seen the shark and was preparing to fight. He opened his arms, his knife in one hand. But the shark wasn't interested in Finn. Bruno had stopped moving but the shark was now making straight for him. The shark's jaws opened. Bruno could see all of his teeth. They were very white and even though Bruno was now terrified, he couldn't help but be impressed with their neatness. Not one out of place. As the shark's jaw started to close around him, a bell rang.

Bruno woke up. His pillow was soaking wet. He'd had a bad dream. Or was it. He looked up at the ceiling and remembered the adventure of the night before. There were voices downstairs. He got up and shook Hamish.

'There's someone at the door, do you know what time it is?'

Hamish, still half asleep, didn't answer and rolled over.

Bruno pulled on his trousers and a jumper and found his watch on the chest of drawers. A quarter to eight. He opened the bedroom door.

A policewoman was standing in the hall below talking to Uncle John who turned when he heard Bruno come out of his room.

'Morning Bruno. I'm afraid someone has stolen Wishful. The police are here taking a statement. In fact you might be able to help, come on down.'

'I don't think so,' answered Bruno defensively. 'Why could I help?'

'Well, you and Hamish have been sailing her this summer. Have you met anyone whilst you have been out?' Uncle John asked.

By this time Bruno had climbed slowly down the stairs and was sitting on the bottom step.

'No.' Bruno's answer wasn't very convincing.

The policewoman frowned. 'Do you know anything that might help us with our enquiries? For instance, have you seen any new boys or girls on the beach that might be interested in the boat?'

Bruno shook his head.

'What about that new boy you met who came fishing with you one day. What was his name?' asked Uncle John.

'Oh, he was only here on holiday for a couple of days,' answered Bruno quickly.

Uncle John nodded. 'Well anyway, it's probably not youngsters that have taken her. I gather she was seen sailing out of the bay and around the point. It must be someone that plans to take her somewhere down the coast.'

The policewoman reached for her hat that she had put down on the chair. 'Well, we'll spread the word. If you get any further information, please let us know.' She put the hat on her head and patted it down to make sure it wouldn't fall off.

'Thank you for your time, Officer.' Uncle John opened the door.

As Bruno watched her walk down the path, he noticed a long green and orange tail trailing out of the back of her hat.

'Oh no.' he groaned putting his hands to his face. 'Pluto!'

He raced up the stairs to wake Hamish, but too late. He heard from outside the house, the most awful shriek and scream. Uncle John had got to the front door by the time Bruno and Hamish had bumped themselves down the stairs on their bottoms and ignored his questions as they raced out of the house and down the path. The police car was parked on the road outside the house, and the policewoman was standing by it with her head in her hands sobbing.

'Are you alright?' asked Hamish cautiously.

The policewoman looked up, Bruno could see she was very upset and her hands were trembling.

'There was a sort of a prehistoric animal inside my hat,' she sobbed. 'It gave me such a fright. I felt this movement on my head and put my hand up. I touched this horrible great cold, wet tail. Oh, it was awful.'

Hamish had already spied the hat. It was lying upside down on the grass a few yards away. It was empty.

'Oh, what happened then?' he asked as calmly as he could, trying to ignore Bruno who was now standing behind the policewoman stifling his laughter by stuffing his hand down his mouth.

'The monster just shot off in that direction. I don't know where, he had millions of legs and ran very quickly.' She was dabbing her eyes now and seemed to have calmed down a bit.

'What's going on?' Uncle John was striding towards them. He was looking at the policewoman.

'Oh, this lady thinks she has seen some sort of prehistoric monster, Uncle John.' Bruno raised his eyes up and down as he tried to get his uncle to understand. 'Apparently it was hiding in her hat, but has now disappeared.'

'Ah, I see.' Uncle John's frown relaxed as he added. 'It was probably our cat. He often hides in hats and is quite grumpy if disturbed.' He winked at Hamish whilst making sure the policewoman didn't see it.

'Did he go across the road, or into another garden?' asked Hamish anxiously.

She was still dabbing her eyes but looked calmer.

'I don't really know. I think he might have crossed the road that way.' She gesticulated with her arm.

Bruno and Hamish ran in the direction she pointed. Across the road, over a bank and into an area of rough grass. They separated, Bruno turning to the right and Hamish walking straight on. Hamish started calling Pluto's name earnestly.

'Over here,' yelled Bruno. 'There's a pond.'

Hamish joined him. It was the size of a large garden pond full of weed and lilies. There was no movement, and Hamish started stirring the edge of the water slowly.

'There he is,' whispered Hamish.

Pluto had appeared out of some long grass on the other side of the pond. He dived into the water and within seconds was walking out of the water next to Hamish.

'You are in trouble, Pluto.' He laughed as he picked him up. 'You'll have to be more choosy about the hats you sleep in or we could all get arrested.'

They were all sitting down to breakfast in the kitchen. Bosun was in the chair by the Aga lying on his back with all four legs in the air. His paws curled over as if ready to grab anything that might come his way. Auntie Moo was obviously very upset about the apparent loss of her boat. Paisley was concentrating hard on her Frosties, hoping that no one would ask her anything, and Hamish had started a conversation with Uncle John about the future of the airport. Bruno looked at his plate miserably wondering how he was going to get Wishful back on the beach without being seen. Finn might do it, but he'd still need help hauling her back up the beach. He needed to find Finn today and talk to him. He glared at Hamish hoping to catch his attention.

'Cornwall is a long way away from London and people want to travel between the two areas.' Uncle John was explaining. Hamish nodded and looked at Bruno, who was now glaring at him and Hamish wondered what he had done wrong. Bruno tilted his head towards the kitchen door.

'I'm going down to the beach to see if we can find anybody that might know what happened to Wishful,' Bruno announced.

'I'll come with you.' Hamish pushed back his chair.

'And me,' cried Paisley, glad to be leaving the watchful eyes of her Uncle and Aunt.

They walked down the path towards the beach, Paisley holding Bruno's hand.

'Whew, that was lucky,' said Bruno. 'Whoever noticed that the boat had been taken simply phoned the police. They obviously didn't know who owned her at that time.'

Paisley added, 'Auntie Moo is very upset about Wishful. Can we put her back?'

'I think so,' answered Bruno seriously. We need to find Finn, and we're not planning to meet him till tomorrow. I wonder when someone will notice that the wind farm mast has disappeared.'

'I know. Why don't we put a message in a bottle for Finn? I'm sure one of the Marinos will find it and pass it on,' said Hamish.

'Yeah,' squealed Paisley. 'Or maybe we could find one of the dolphins and ask them to tell Finn.'

Bruno squinted at the sun and frowned. 'I think the bottle is a good idea. We've got nothing to lose anyway. The only way to find one of the dolphins is by boat, and that's the one thing we now don't have. Let's go back to the house and see if we can find a bottle.'

Before they got to the house, they passed a litterbin and propped up against it was a carrier bag full of mostly empty bottles obviously left there from a beach party. Hamish pulled out one that had a cork and they set off back to the house to find pen and paper.

FINN,
WE NEED YOUR HELP. PLEASE COME TO THE ROCKS AS SOON AS YOU CAN. BRUNO

Hamish rolled up the message, slipped it into the bottle and pushed the cork on. He spent some time doing this as the cork was very tight, but at least it would keep the water out once he had finished, he thought.

The tide was going out and Bruno thought that the bottle would need to be launched on the West side of the Bay so that the tide would take it over the top of Marino. They set off to walk around the bay. Apart from a few people walking their dogs, there was no one else around. It was still early. A quarter to nine. Most people didn't arrive for at least another half an hour.

'Look,' said Hamish under his breath.

Ahead of them but on the road, three men were standing looking out to sea. One of them was looking through binoculars. Bruno strained his ears but he was too far away to hear what they were saying. The man with the binoculars was shaking his head and handed the binoculars to one of the other men. The third man pulled his mobile out of his pocket. All of them looked agitated.

As they approached, Bruno heard the voice of the man with the phone. He had raised his voice and was shouting something about organising a boat.

Bruno looked at Hamish and Paisley and grinned. They walked on by and collapsed on a rock at the end of the beach.

'Well, I think they've seen it now,' laughed Paisley.

'Yes, and they're obviously going to go and see what's happened,' said Bruno. 'Throw the bottle Hamish, as hard as you can.'

Hamish waded out until the water was just below his shorts. It was cold and it took his breath away as he pulled his arm right back over his shoulder and then hurled the bottle as hard as he could out into the surf. Luckily it landed just outside of the surf and within minutes they could see it had been caught by the tide and was moving away from them.

'Good, we'll have to spend the day on our rocks. I suggest we go there now and one of us can go back and get the fishing gear. Paisley, do you want to stay with us or go back to the house.'

'I want to see Botolph and Osquirt,' answered Paisley slowly, looking at her brother as if she were asking for a treat.

'Well, I can't make that happen, but if we swim around the rocks, they may come anyway. Let's go.'

CHAPTER 17 – The Sea is her own master

Finn had explained to Bruno that the Gillanders made most of their money fishing and selling shells. They owned two large fishing vessels, which they mainly used for transportation of building materials and items for the Marino home. Fishing was easy for the Gillanders. They would either catch a large shark (as Talon had shown the boys) or set a net close by to Marino and when a shoal of fish arrived, they would see it and simply close the net around them. This way, there was no wastage, no catching fish they didn't want, or any danger of getting a dolphin or seal or bird stuck in the net. They would then hoist this onto the boat and take it to Oldquay Harbour.

Most of the children helped to earn their keep by collecting shells. Because they were able to swim to depths that most ordinary people cannot reach without an oxygen tank, they found unusual shells that weren't on sale in most shops and were therefore able to get a good price for them.

Gupwort's cousin, Penmellyn, or Pen for short, was master of one of the fishing boats GILL 1, and on the morning after the mast was pulled down, he was instructed by Polperro to go into Oldquay harbour to see if there was any news. The sea was blue and Pen and his daughter, Coral, who was the team leader in the game of Dolphin Rush, were sitting at the back of the boat sunning themselves. GILL was fitted with an autopilot and Pen had set this up so that the boat could steer herself towards the entrance of the harbour.

'I can see something in the water over there. It looks like a bottle with something in it,' said Coral.

'Probably a message in a bottle,' said Pen laughing. In all his days at sea, he'd never found a message in a bottle although it was understood that in the olden days, many messages were found. Pen went forward to the wheelhouse, and pulled back on the throttle. The boat slowed to a stop beside the bottle. Coral leant over the side of the boat and grabbed it.

'There is,' she cried excitedly. 'There's a message.' She tried to pull the cork off the top, but eventually handed it to her father. He pulled out the note and handed it back to her.

FINN, WE NEED YOUR HELP. PLEASE COME TO THE ROCKS AS SOON AS YOU CAN.
BRUNO

'This is from one of the Leylander boys that helped in the mast operation last night,' said Pen.

'Yes, I remember him from the game, shall I take it to Marino?' replied Coral

'I suppose you had better, it sounds urgent. I'll wait here,' answered Pen.

Coral dived overboard and was gone within a second. Penn settled back to wait for her return and noticed a boat approaching from the direction of the Harbour. It was a small, fast workboat with equipment on the back of it. Pen realised it was pointing towards him and wondered whether they would be asking about the mast. Anyway, he had his answers ready. They were soon alongside.

'Hi, we were just wondering if you had seen anything odd happening around here this morning.' The man had on a blue suit and tie and looked very out of place standing on the deck of a boat.

'No, what kind of thing do you mean?' answered Penn lightly.

'Well, you may have heard. There is a plan to build a new windfarm out here and a mast was put up over there, just to the Northwest of us, last month. It seems to have disappeared overnight. We can't understand it.'

Pen shrugged. 'The sea is her own master.

She can make things happen. If she wants to destroy something, she will. You can't mess with the sea, you know.'

'Er, well yes, I see, but I don't think the sea could have uprooted an 80 metre mast that was driven 7 metres into the seabed rock.' The man looked at Pen seriously. 'We believe it was pulled down by someone or something!'

'Don't know about that. I haven't heard or seen anyone out here this morning. I left Oldquay yesterday afternoon and spent most of my time since, up East of here towards Ladstow.'

At that moment, Coral popped her head over the side of the deck and pulled herself on board.

'Oh, Coral, there you are. These gentlemen are looking for a mast which seems to have come down in the night,' Pen said nervously.

Coral nodded. 'That'll be the sea, I expect. If she doesn't like something, she gets rid of it. You can't control the sea, you know.'

The man sighed and turned to look at another well-dressed man standing behind him.

'It seems we're not getting anywhere here.' He looked back at Penmellyn. 'Well thanks for your time. If you do hear anything, could you contact us? Here is my card.' Pen took the card and waved. They watched the men get into the boat and turn towards Oldquay.

153

'So Coral, did you find Finn?'

'Yes, he's going to look for Bruno now. If it's ok with you, I said I'd go and meet him at the rocks in case they need some help.'

Penmellyn smiled. 'Yes, you go. They have been very good to us over this windfarm business. It would be nice if we could repay them. I'll see you back at Marino later on.' Coral disappeared back into the water.

CHAPTER 18 – Wishful is returned

Hamish was sitting on the rocks whilst Bruno and Paisley went back to the house to get the fishing rods. He was thinking about Wishful and wondering how they could get her back to the beach without getting into trouble themselves. He had almost forgotten about the reason for all this. The wind farm mast was down, but so far, no one had said anything about it. At least that meant no one connected them with anything.

'Hello again. Do you remember me?' It was Coral. She had swum up to the rocks and appeared out of nowhere.

'Yes, you were the best player in the Dolphin Rush,' answered Hamish shyly. 'Do you know where Finn is?'

Coral nodded. 'On his way here. I found your message in the bottle and passed it on to Finn. I wondered if you needed any help. That's why I'm here!' she said proudly, as if she would be very useful in any emergency.

Hamish turned his head towards a splashing sound behind him. Finn pulled himself out of the water and sat down on the rocks.

'So what's the problem?' he said immediately.

'On our way home early this morning, someone had called the police and told them that Wishful was missing.' Hamish explained. 'It wasn't Auntie Moo. Probably someone that saw us go out. A police car was waiting on the beach, so we took the boat to the cave and left her there. We want to get her back without being caught.'

Bruno and Paisley arrived back with the rods and sat down on the rocks with the others.

'Um, difficult,' said Finn. 'If we put her back for you tonight, that will look very odd in the morning. How about we bring her round to this bay in broad daylight. The tide will be coming in. Coral and I can manoeuvre her out of the cave and with the help of Osquirt and Botolph we can push her from underneath. You can pretend you see her bobbing about in the bay and swim out to her when she comes in close enough. That way, people will assume that whoever stole her, abandoned her.'

Paisley clapped her hands. 'It's a good plan.' She beamed at Bruno who was still wearing his worried frown as he said. 'The only worry would be coming out of the cave. You need to make sure there is no one else around and you won't be able to do that if you're underwater.'

'What if we stand guard,' Hamish suggested. We can stand on the cliff top and make sure no one comes around from either bays on the right or left. Once you're out of the cave we can run back here and swim out to the boat when you bring her in.'

'Brilliant,' Finn nodded his head at Hamish. 'Let's agree hand signals then. I suggest that one of you raises both arms above your head when the coast is clear. Okay?'

The boys nodded. Bruno let out a large sigh, relieved that they were going to get the boat back without being suspected.

There were no other boats in sight and Bruno and Hamish were standing as close to the edge of the cliff as they dared, above the opening to the cave which seemed to be miles down. They could make out a brown dot in the water and realised it was Finn ready to take instructions. The boys looked around to check that the coast was clear and raised their arms. Finn disappeared.

Within a few seconds, Wishful appeared as if from nowhere and slowly moved left away from the cliff out to sea. Bruno thought she looked rather majestic moving slowly through the water without anyone aboard. A bit like a ghost ship.

'What do you think you're doing?' shouted a voice suddenly from behind. Bruno recognised it.

'Wha.. What do you mean?' answered Bruno turning to find Uncle John just behind him. The surprise of his voice had made Bruno jump and he quickly lowered his arms.

'Were you two intending to dive off the cliff at this height?' asked Uncle John looking angrily at the two boys. 'You must be mad, and you've got Paisley with you.' He grabbed hold of Bruno and shook his shoulder. 'What are you thinking, Bruno?'

'Well Sir, we were just wondering what it would be like really,' answered Bruno, his thoughts racing around his head looking for something to say. 'Of course, it was only just a thought.'

But Uncle John wasn't listening. He was staring out to sea at the small boat moving slowly but surely towards Lusty Glaze beach.

'There she is,' he cried. 'There she is.'

'Where?' shouted all three of them pretending they hadn't seen her earlier.

'Just down there, now moving towards the beach. Come on.' Uncle John started to run down the cliff path back towards the beach, followed by Hamish, and then Paisley and Bruno who was talking to Paisley between breaths.

'Don't mention Finn or the dolphins to Uncle John, Paisley,' he told her firmly.

'I'm not a baby, you know,' answered Paisley crossly. 'I can keep a secret.'

By the time Hamish caught up with Uncle John, he was standing at the water's edge taking off his shoes and socks. Bruno arrived panting.

'Let us go. We've got our swims on and you haven't. We can bring her in, can't we Hamish?'

Uncle John looked out to sea. Wishful was moving closer into the beach.

'Okay, but Paisley stays with me, and if you get tired, tread water for a while.'

Before he had finished the sentence, Bruno and Hamish had dived in and were swimming like crazy towards the boat, which had stopped, moving. They went around the back of the boat so they couldn't be seen and met Finn who had just surfaced.

'We nearly had a problem,' explained Bruno. 'Uncle John is on the beach, he was about to come out here.'

'Its okay, I wouldn't have surfaced if there was someone I didn't know. I'll find you on the rocks tomorrow. Bye.' He was gone.

Hamish and Bruno heaved themselves over Wishful's small transom at the back of the boat, and Hamish unfurled the jib. This would be enough to get them to the beach. He looked at Bruno. 'Well done captain,' and saluted as he did so. Bruno smiled back.

CHAPTER 19
Windfarm Developers get cold feet

Auntie Moo was grilling some bacon for breakfast when the boys appeared in the kitchen. The Oldquay daily news was sitting on the kitchen table and the headline stared out at them.

MYSTERY OF WINDMAST
DISAPPEARANCE

Hamish nudged Bruno, and they both sat down.

'Isn't Paisley with you? She seems to be very tired lately, I hope she's not going down with something.'

Bruno, could you go up and see if she's all right and tell her that breakfast is ready.' Auntie Moo looked at Bruno quickly before she carefully lifted a rasher of bacon off the grill onto a freshly buttered piece of bread. Bosun was sitting by her foot and reached up to try and get the bacon off the spoon as it passed above her head. Auntie Moo ignored this and continued to serve up the rest of the bacon while Bosun hissed and walked away, jumping onto one of the kitchen chairs.

'Did you sleep all right Hamish. You look

quite tired? Are you all up to something I don't know about? It seems to me that you've not been sleeping properly.'

'Oh no, Auntie Moo. It's just that hot weather makes me tired. That's all.' Hamish smiled at her hoping that would be the end of the conversation.

Bruno appeared with Paisley who had obviously just woken up and wanted to sit on the chair that Bosun had taken.

'Just shoo him off Paisley,' instructed Auntie Moo firmly. 'He won't hurt you, he'll just hiss and growl.'

Paisley put out her hand to push him off the chair and Bosun immediately retaliated with a loud hiss and growl that made Paisley take a step back.

'Enough, you naughty cat,' shouted Auntie Moo. Grabbing the newspaper and rolling it up. She brought it down hard on the tabletop and the noise was enough to frighten Bosun, who jumped off the chair and ran out of the room.

Bruno and Hamish stared at the newspaper in her hand. They desperately wanted to read it, but it was still rolled up, Auntie Moo put it on the mantelpiece behind the sink.

'Did I see something about the new windfarm in the paper?' asked Hamish lightly.

'Yes, it looks like they've lost their test mast

out there somewhere. All sounds very odd. One day its there and the next its not. The paper says the windfarm developers are very upset as it cost a lot of money and until they find out what happened to it, the insurance company won't pay for it.' She passed the newspaper to Bruno

'I suppose they'll put another one in its place, won't they,' asked Hamish pretending not to be particularly interested.

'I'm not sure. They believe it might be a problem building a windfarm in that area after all. They think that the seabed has some unusual rock formations, and whatever caused these might have made the seabed unstable.'

'Wow,' said Bruno over enthusiastically. 'So it might not happen at all then?'

'You sound as if you're pleased. I thought you wanted to use it as a part of your school project?' Auntie Moo joined them at the table.

'Well yes, but it will change the view quite a lot, won't it?' Paisley chipped in.

'Yes, and they don't need another one.' Bruno concluded.

'Well, I'm amazed at you. Who would have thought you were all under 12 years old. Where's the spirit in you, where's the adventure of having something new and different. 'Auntie Moo exclaimed.

Bruno winked at Paisley. 'I guess we're just

too boring and unadventurous.' He sighed as he said it to give the sentence extra meaning.

Auntie Moo looked at her nephew. What a strange boy. One minute, so carefree, and brave, and the next, careful and serious.

She shrugged. 'Well, if you've finished your breakfast, you can all get down. What are your plans today.' Bosun appeared through the doorway, and Paisley pushed back her chair, patting her knees. Bosun jumped up and settled into the 'v' between her small legs. 'We're going to the rocks to meet Finn,' she whispered absentmindedly as if talking to Bosun.

'Who's Finn?' asked Auntie Moo. I thought he'd gone home weeks ago.

'Oh, er, yes.' Hamish scowled at Paisley.' He's down for a few days and we met up with him yesterday whilst looking for Wishful.' Paisley nodded realising she had said something she shouldn't.

'Why don't you invite him back here for lunch? I should like to meet him.' Auntie Moo said kindly.

'I don't know if he'll be able to today. He's usually quite busy.' Bruno answered quickly.

'Well, if he wants to come, there will be plenty of food. Off you go then, I'll see you later.'

Bruno had picked up the newspaper as he left the table and put it under his shirt so as not to catch his Aunt's attention. Once they were clear of the house, he pulled it out.

"Windfarm developers fear the chosen site for the windfarm could be unstable. Mystery surrounds the disappearance of the test wind mast erected 10 day ago, which was drilled 7 metres down into the seabed. Project manager, Peter Brewer says 'The mast broke off at the point it entered the seabed; something must have shaken it very hard. We believe it could only have been an earth tremor and this puts a question mark over the whole development. We will be making a full investigation."

'Yes,' shouted Bruno, punching the air.

'What does tremor mean?' asked Paisley quietly. She was still waiting for Bruno to tell her off.

'Well,' answered Bruno, pulling himself up to his full height. 'I'm not exactly sure, but I think it means that the sea bed is wobbly so nothing will stay fixed in it.'

They walked on down to the beach and climbed up onto the rocks to wait for Finn. They didn't have to wait long. Finn appeared with a large live Cornish crab, which he offered to Hamish.

'Would you like this for lunch?' he asked

'Yuck,' said Paisley. 'I would not.'

'No, but Auntie Moo and Uncle John would love it. Oh and you've been invited to come for lunch,' said Hamish.

'Hang on! Aren't crabs your friends?' asked Bruno. His frown creeping across his forehead.

Finn smiled. 'Well, we have our own crab family who are sort of pets really. And then there is the lobster family - the ones you saw biting off the rope around Catapus. But then we have many friends of the sea. We have to eat though, so we catch fish and shell fish.'

'How do you know if this is one of your pets though?' Paisley whispered.

'Our crabs and lobsters spend most of their time in Marino. They have a ready made protection system from everything that might eat them, so they're not going to risk going outside to be caught,' Finn answered seriously. 'You ought to try it, they are delicious.'

Hamish was trying to hold the crab that was writhing around and trying to get hold of his arm with his pincers.

'We've got good news.' Bruno unfolded the newspaper excitedly. 'The developers think there might be a problem with the seabed and they might not go ahead.'

'Wow, wait till Polperro hears that. He'll be

doing aquasaults.' He looked at Bruno's quizzical face. 'Oh, you know, somersaults underwater.'

'That would be fun. I wish I had some aquadaptors here so I could try it.' Bruno answered.

'Why don't I get Osquirt to fetch some for you all and we could go for a dolphin race?' Finn said cheerfully.

'Oh yes please.' Paisley jumped up and turned her head to look out to sea searching for the dolphins.

Bruno nodded. 'I can't think of a better way to end our holiday, unless of course, I could be allowed to ride one of the sharks instead.' A quizzical look crossed his face.

Finn laughed. 'Next year, my friend, next year!'

My thanks to Jan Hartley-Trigg for her
time and advice.

Made in the USA
Charleston, SC
05 April 2016